Charmian was appalled at Randolph Heriot's statements and told him, "Pray do not strain your charitable instincts on my behalf, sir. I would sooner starve in the gutter than turn to *you* for support. As for claiming kinship, I would rather claim it with that broken-down retainer whom you describe so scathingly, for he is more of the true gentleman that *you* have shown yourself. You are the rudest, horridest wretch that it has ever been my misfortune to meet, and I can only trust that our acquaintance will be of the briefest."

But everything in life is subject to change, as Charmian would discover . . .

Fawcett Crest Books
by Mira Stables:

THE BYRAM SUCCESSION 23558-0 $1.50

FRIENDS AND RELATIONS 24235-8 $1.75

HONEY-POT 23915-2 $1.75

MARRIAGE ALLIANCE 23929-2 $1.75

STRANGER WITHIN THE GATES 23402-9 $1.50

THE SWYNDEN NECKLACE 23270-0 $1.50

FRIENDS
AND
RELATIONS

Mira Stables

FAWCETT COVENTRY • NEW YORK

FRIENDS AND RELATIONS

Published by Fawcett Coventry Books, a unit of CBS
Publications, the Consumer Publishing Division of CBS
Inc., by arrangement with Robert Hale Limited.

ISBN: 0-449-50019-5

THIS BOOK CONTAINS THE COMPLETE TEXT OF
THE ORIGINAL HARDCOVER EDITION.

Printed in the United States of America

First Fawcett Coventry printing: December 1979

10   9   8   7   6   5   4   3   2   1

ONE

"CHARMIAN!"

The voice was little more than a husky whisper, fretful with weakness.

The girl at the window turned swiftly, striving to mask her own anxiety with an air of cheerful competence, and took the sick woman's wasted hand in her own warm young one.

"Did you have a nice refreshing nap, Mama? Shall I make your tea now? I could enjoy a cup myself, and the hot drink might soothe your poor throat."

The invalid's assent was languid but when the tray was brought in she drank the tea thirstily, though she did no more than nibble at a little cake. As the girl set the scarcely tasted food aside she said urgently, "You will come back as soon as you have carried the tray down? There is much that we must talk of."

Charmian might have said that she always *did*

come back to her mother's room as soon as her various domestic preoccupations permitted; that she scamped her other duties in order to spend more time with the invalid. She contented herself with arranging the pillows more comfortably and making up the fire before she left the room. During the long weeks of nursing she had learned to accept both unreasonable demands and implied criticism with patience.

Her return caused the sick woman to try to raise herself on the pillows which brought on a fit of coughing. It left her exhausted, the handkerchief that she held to her lips ominously stained. But she refused to rest. The doctor had tacitly admitted that her time was short, and she had that on her mind, she whispered, that she must confide without further delay.

It seemed best to let her unburden herself though the effort must take heavy toll of her small reserves of strength. Charmian said in subdued tones, "Dearest Mama. Tell me if you must. But I think perhaps I have already guessed. Can you not spare yourself the pain of making such a disclosure when you are so weak?"

A flicker of sheer amazement stirred the pallid features. "You *cannot* have guessed," Mrs. Tracy said, irritability lending strength to her voice. "Surmise you may have indulged, but the truth is too deep hidden. Tell me, pray, what imaginings you have been nourishing in your idle hours."

There had been few enough of those, thought Charmian ruefully. Sickness had wrought a sad change in Mama. In health she had been a devoted parent, firm, but kind withal. Who would have dreamed that she would turn into this querulous complaining creature who did not scruple to aim bitter shafts at the girl who tended her as well as youth and experience permitted? Charmian had flushed to the roots of her hair but she met her mother's eyes squarely. There were no words to soften what she had to say, but at least it was a relief to have it out in the open at last.

"You have never spoken to me about my father. For several years now—certainly before I left school—I have thought that perhaps I was born out of wedlock."

There was no denial. The still face on the pillows awaited further disclosures. Charmian said slowly, "It seemed to be the only answer to the peculiarities of my situation. If we were not precisely wealthy, we were at least well to pass. At home we enjoyed every comfort. I was sent to a very select seminary and the bills were never questioned. Dancing, riding, music—every imaginable extra—I took them all. Yet when I left school you made no push to launch me into society. By now most of my friends are married. Mary Swain has two babies. And at that time—when I left school, I mean—you were well and did not need my attendance upon you. If there was no slur on my birth, why did you make no attempt to marry me off? Most parents do, when a girl has been given an expensive education."

The pale lips were actually faintly smiling. "Quite astute. And not so far from the truth. No point now in further concealment. Yes, I *did* have a daughter, born out of wedlock, though at the time I believed myself to be married. But she died in infancy. Sometimes I have wondered if you were sent to comfort my loneliness. For why did no one come forward to claim you? Yet there were times, too," she added broodingly, "when I almost hated you, just for being alive, while my precious Melanie was cold in her grave. Nay, child, never look so distressed. This is a time for the truth. You have been a good and dutiful daughter to me and the least I can do for you is to put you into possession of such facts as are known to me. Nor need you fear for the future when I am gone. Provision has been made for you."

It was the longest connected speech that she had uttered for several days and it had wearied her. She lay some time with closed eyes. Charmian was well aware of her need for sleep—the doctor had stressed it repeatedly—but for once concern for the invalid was swept aside by her own shock and dismay. She said impetuously, "But if I am not your child, Mama, who am I?"

The heavy lids lifted. Mama—to Charmian she would always be Mama—said gently, "My dear, I do not know."

There was a heavy silence. Then the sick woman

went on, "You were left in my care by your nurse. She did not come back, and no one ever claimed you. She was on her way to London, taking you to relatives. Grandparents, we thought, but she spoke with a strange accent so we were not sure. And now I must sleep. The full story must wait, though there is no more that I can tell you about your parentage."

It was long before Charmian slept. The shock of Mama's disclosure over-ruled the demands of a weary body. But after tossing restlessly for what seemed like hours, her imagination a prey to every kind of conjecture about her strange history—or rather her lack of it—she came gradually to some kind of acceptance. Fretting would do no good. Time and diligent search might eventually reveal what kind of people she was sprung from. Meanwhile she must count herself fortunate that she had fallen into such kindly hands. At least certain matters which had long puzzled her were now explained. The total lack of resemblance between Mama and herself, for instance. For Mama was lily fair, and before she took ill she had been a Juno of a woman, while Charmian had brown eyes and golden-brown curls and, to her sad disappointment, was small and slight, with no claims at all to the luscious feminine curves that were so fashionable. Mama was gracious, controlled and dignified in ways and speech. Charmian was quick-silver, with a bubbling gaiety and zest for living that had been sadly dashed of late. She had always supposed herself to resemble the unknown Papa of whom Mama never spoke, and in her foolish teens had woven many an absurd romance about him, consoling herself in this childish fashion for the slur which she believed to stain her birth.

She recalled these flights of fancy now with an indulgent little smile, as an adult remembers outgrown playthings. Whatever her parentage, it was improbable that her father was the Prince or the Royal Duke of her dreams! She pondered long over Mama's personal tragedy, hearing again that bitter little confession—"At times I almost hated you, just for being alive." It did much to explain moods that had hurt and bewildered her. On a vow that never again would she permit herself to feel resentment when Mama spoke crossly or appeared unjust, Charmian drifted at last into uneasy slumber.

It was a vow impossible of keeping, of course. Mama, next morning, was in her most difficult mood. Charmian could do nothing right. When she brushed out the long fair hair she was accused of roughness and undue haste. The gruel that she had prepared so carefully was too sweet. Mama was not a baby to be coaxed with sugared pap. And when her eyes strayed to the window, where a brisk October gale was rattling the fallen leaves against the casement, she was heartless and selfish, wanting only to be out of doors enjoying herself, regardless of the invalid's sufferings. Charmian, who was naturally impatient to hear the rest of the story, found it very difficult to preserve a tranquil demeanour. As for making any enquiry about her own arrival into Mama's life, it was more than she dare venture.

It was not until the darkening that a much-tried girl, drawing the curtains across the rain-spattered windows, murmured tentatively that they were very snug and cozy in the firelit room with the raw autumnal night shut out, and inadvertently touched off the spring of reminiscence for which she had sought all day.

"You do not rémember any other home, of course," sighed Mama pensively. "You were scarce a year old when we brought you here—or so we reckoned. But the first home that I can recall was Aunt Caroline's house in Williamsburg. So very different! The summers, long and sunny and hot. And the scent of the roses! It was in June that I met my Philip. I never smell roses without remembering. He had been wounded—badly wounded—and when the army moved on they left the wounded and the prisoners behind. Philip had tried to make his own way after them, all dazed as he was with fever and his injuries, and Aunt Caroline and I found him by the roadside. Naturally we took him in and nursed him. Aunt was always a Loyalist, and I could never understand the rights and wrongs of the struggle. Why should I care that Philip wore a red coat? I knew that my father was fighting with Washington, but I had never seen him since he had left me with Aunt Caroline when I was just turned seven. If I *had* any politics I sided with my aunt rather than my father. But in those days we mostly left such matters to the gentlemen. When a girl is seventeen she cares more for a young man's appearance and bearing than for the colour of his coat. Philip was handsome even when he was fever-thin, and as his health came back I fell more and more deeply in love with him. Even in sickness he was gentle and courteous. With returning vigour he had an engaging charm that I found irresistible. Aunt Caroline loved him, too. Even the authorities turned a blind eye on the fact that we were sheltering a Britisher. Though that was rather because his wits were still clouded, my poor Philip."

She felt silent, re-living those happy days when all had seemed so simple and straightforward. Charmian, who was beginning to feel that her own wits were clouded as she strove to sort out this jumble of apparently unrelated facts, waited respectfully, but when Mama made no move to resume her story she said timidly, "Whereabouts *is* Williamsburg, Mama? I have never heard you speak of it before, and I cannot recall meeting anyone else who lived there."

"I really don't know what they teach girls nowadays," sighed Mama. "When I was young we were educated at home and—but no matter for that. It is in America, goose, in Virginia. And a very happy girlhood I passed there with Aunt Caroline, despite the hardships of war. All the young men were gone off to fight, either on one side or the other, so there were few parties and no beaux. But we kept ourselves amused and cheerful. As a family we had no one involved in the fighting except Papa, and he was little more than a name to me since he had married again and handed me over to Aunt Caroline. The war did not seem very real until General Cornwallis occupied Williamsburg during his withdrawal of Yorktown. Even then, although we were frightened after the dreadful tales that we had heard, it was not so very bad. They took all our stores, of course—armies always do—and such horses as hadn't been hidden, but there were no shellings or burnings or hangings as there had been at other places. So you see I had no personal cause to hate the British and found it all too easy to fall in love with one particular Englishman."

"And you and Aunt Caroline nursed him back to health," prompted Charmian presently.

Mama shook her head. "Not entirely. Though his wounds healed and he gained strength daily, he still could not remember anything except that his name was Philip. And we had burned his uniform in the early days when we were still trying to keep him hidden so we could not even discover what regiment he had belonged to. It troubled him a good deal at times, wondering about his family in England who doubtless thought him dead, but since he was as deep in love as I was we were mostly too happy to grieve. He was a great help to our feminine household. We were all agreed that he must come of farming stock, such a knack as he had with animals. I think he would have been content to settle in Virginia, but Aunt thought that we should go to England and try if we could not trace his family. He might have a mother breaking her heart for loss, she said, and, as she had just inherited this house, she suggested that we should come and look over it and, at the same time, set on foot enquiries about Philip. In fact she made it a condition for her consent to our marriage—and little guessed what sorrow it would bring. She had thought of a grieving mother. None of us had thought that Philip might be married and himself a father. He was so young. And surely he must have remembered a wife if he truly loved her."

Her voice faltered and died. And this time Charmian could not bring herself to intrude on that sorrowful reverie.

It was fortunate that Susan, who had known Mama ever since she had gone to live with Aunt Caroline, was well acquainted with the whole story and, now that the secret was out, quite willing to amplify the disjointed snippets that Charmian got from Mama. Mama would move backward and forward in time as the mood took her and soon had Charmian thoroughly muddled as to the sequence of events, but thanks to Susan she was able to piece the story together.

"I'll not name names, miss, until your Mama chooses to do so in his own good time," stipulated

Susan. And with this proviso launched into brisk narrative. Aunt Caroline, she said, had been wishful to return to England for several reasons. Now that the war was as good as over and it was plain that there would be no resumption of British rule in Virginia, she was unsettled. The inheritance of the house had seemed like an omen drawing her back to her homeland. Moreover she was deeply curious about Philip's background.

"Anyone could see he was gentry born," Susan explained. "Not just the high-bred looks of him but his speech and his ways. And book learning, too. Reckon she hoped he was related to some great family and that maybe she'd see her niece a ladyship. If only she'd let well alone! Though I s'pose it'd have had to come out sooner or later. Mr. Philip cared little enough. Wholly taken up with the news that Miss Bel—your Mama I *should* say—was in the family way, and that pleased and excited he'd no thought for anything else. In the end Miss Caroline lost patience and went off to London herself to see about making enquiries at army headquarters."

She paused as though wondering how far her confidences should go, and devoted all her attention to the apples she was paring.

"I know that he was already married," volunteered Charmian. "Married, and the father of a child. Mama told me that herself."

Susan sighed. "Seems he was always army mad, but he was the only son and his father was against it. Said he must first marry and beget an heir, for there was a title and estates to consider. And that's just what he did, and him scarce twenty! Not that I think he was unwilling," she added reflectively. "By all accounts she was a nice little piece, the girl that he married. They'd grown up as playmates and liked each other well enough. Must have been like two children playing at grown-ups—her just seventeen and scarce out of the schoolroom."

The apple pie went into the oven and she began to beat eggs for a custard as she took up the story again. "She had her baby within the year, a fine healthy boy, and then Mr. Philip held his Papa to his promise and was off to join his regiment, which was sent to America before his brave scarlet coat had fairly settled itself to his shoulders. Maybe if he'd been just an ordinary sort of man they'd never have traced his family and he and Miss Bel would have lived out their lives happily enough. But he wasn't. He *did* come of titled folk, just as Miss Caroline had hoped, and her lawyer had no trouble at all in tracing him. There'd been enquiries made after him already. His lordship—Mr. Philip's father —came down himself to identify him. He was kind enough. But there could be no denying that Miss Bel was no true wife, however innocent she was. It was all hushed up of course. Nobody wanted a scandal. There was money settled on Miss Bel for the sake of the child, and Mr. Philip's father took him home. I'll not forget the look in Miss Bel's eyes as she watched them go. She loved him truly, miss, and a sore price she paid for it. Just about killed Miss Caroline, too. She picked up a bit after the baby was born. A pretty little thing she was, but always frail. Miss Caroline doted on her and nearly went out of her mind when the poor mite took ill and pined. Never pulled up again after the baby's death. The lung sickness, just like your Mama now. If you ask me, Miss Charmian, they're a sickly stock and you can be thankful it's not *their* blood that runs in your veins, for all that Miss Bel's been so good to you."

Charmian nodded soberly. "So very good," she said. "I can never thank her enough or begin to repay her. But since that first time she has never spoken of how I came into her keeping. You were there, weren't you, Susan. Won't you tell me about it?"

Susan stirred her custard carefully. "Yes, I was there. And never so frightened since we'd crossed the ocean. Snow, miss. A thing to which I wasn't much accustomed. Great whirling clouds of it, so's you couldn't see and scarcely breathe, and piling up in the hedges in deep drifts. Myself, I'd never have chosen to travel in such weather but Miss Bel was always on the fidget those days. Never stayed anywhere long. We'd been in Dover—she'd a fancy for old, historic places and would wander about with her sketch book in the bitter wind when I'm sure her fingers must have been too frozen to hold the pencil. So next we must be off to London. Maybe some new clothes in pretty colours would pluck up her spirits—she was tired of wearing black. Well, I'd nothing to say against that. In fact I thought it was a good idea. And it wasn't actually snowing when we set off, though the guard on the Mail warned us that more falls were threatened."

She shivered at the mere memory and poured the thickened custard into a bowl. "There was just the one other passenger," she went on, filling the pan with water, "and an odd sort of creature she was. A big strapping woman in rough country clothes, carrying a baby. More the sort to be travelling in the stage you'd have thought, and certainly not like any nursemaid that I'd ever seen. I thought the baby was hers until we got talking and she said she was taking it to relations in London. Pleasant enough she spoke but with a queer sort of brogue. Which was why I couldn't be sure if it was grandparents she was taking you to. And she'd no notion at all how to handle a baby. Miss Bel hadn't paid much heed to her until you began to cry and she couldn't quiet you. Your little hands and feet were blue with cold and the shawl you were wrapped in was thin and much darned. Miss Bel snuggled you up inside her fur cape. The silly creature wanted to feed you with some cold meat that she had with her! Luckily you went to sleep as soon as you were warmed. But it was just about then that the snow began again. Before long the horses were down to a walk and we could scarcely see the road for blowing snow. Once we stuck in a drift and the guard got a farmer to come and drag us out. Six great horses it took. But there was nowhere for us to shelter. The farmer said his wife was sick of the scarlet fever and could not take us in. There was a small inn four or five miles down the road, he said. Country miles I reckon they were, or maybe it was the cold and the whirling snow that made them so long. Anyway we never reached the inn because we stuck again, and this time there was no convenient farmer to pull us out. The guard and the driver did what they could, but then, to add to our troubles, the driver had some kind of a fit and collapsed. It was your strange attendant who helped the guard to lift the poor man into the body of the coach and who chafed his half frozen limbs until he showed signs of returning consciousness. The guard then announced that *his* first duty was to see that the mails were carried to their destination, in which belief your nursemaid supported him, declaring that her brother had been a post-boy and so she knew what was right and proper. Miss Bel protested that he could not leave us to the mercy of the elements, but he said we should be safe enough if we kept to the coach and wrapped ourselves warmly. When he explained that he would take the horses and ride ahead with the mailbags, your nurse volunteered to go with him, if we would take charge of you, and make sure that help was sent back at once. We did our best to dissuade her but she was quite determined. And to see her wrap a shawl about her head and kilt up her skirts to climb on one of the horses, you could tell she knew what she was about. Handled a horse far better than she'd handled an infant. But courage and determination weren't enough, poor soul. Somehow they lost the road. They must have wandered in circles until the horses were exhausted and then set out to walk. Their bodies were found a week later when the snow melted."

Charmian gave a little gasp of shock and pity. Mama's revelations had not prepared her for such a tragedy and Susan's brisk, matter-of-fact manner had given little warning.

"And you never found out who she was?"

Susan shook her head. "No. There was some talk of a boat that had put into Dover and landed a woman passenger, but no one could say for sure if she was carrying a baby. The boat had a Cornish crew—foreigners the Dover fishermen called them —smugglers and privateers and worse. Nobody would admit to knowing anything about them for all Miss Bel's enquiries. In the end she gave up the idea of going to London and brought you back here. But there was one queer-like thing. Though your shawl was so miserably thin and your dress was of rough material, not to say shabby and dirty, yet when we undressed you—next day that way, when we were rescued—your little shift and flannel and petticoats were of the finest materials, beautifully sewn and embroidered. And round your neck was an old silver amulet. Did your Mama tell you? One side of it had been chased in some design, but with much wear there was little of that to be seen. The other side was plain, and across it someone had scratched with a nail or a pin the one word Charmian. That's how you came by your name, miss. Though whether it really is your name or not, there's no telling. But I know your Mama saved the little clothes and the medallion in case some day they might help you to prove who you really are. You should ask her to show them to you, one of her good days."

TWO

CHARMIAN SCANNED THE AWKWARD stilted phrases that she had achieved at the last attempt and flung down the pen in exasperation. It was no good. She crumpled the sheets and tossed them into the hearth. To be writing to a stranger must always be difficult. When one had to deal with such intimate matters it became impossible. She thrust ink-stained fingers through unruly curls and rested her head on her hands, gazing into the glowing heart of the fire as though it might bring inspiration. But all she could picture was Mama's face. How Mama would have scolded to see Charmian with her elbows propped on the table in that inelegant attitude! And how indignant Mama would be if she knew what her adopted daughter was planning. Though she had been more like her old self during the closing days of her life, the girl had never ventured to voice her doubts about the propriety of accepting the inheritance of which Mama had spoken. In any case it would have been unkind to have done so, since Mama obviously derived a good deal of comfort from the knowledge that she was leaving her well provided for.

Susan had told her bluntly that she must be all about in her head. To be refusing what was rightfully and legally hers for some ridiculous quirk of conscience was the height of folly. "Plain to be seen that *you've* never known what it is to want," she had grumbled with the frankness of an old and trusted servant. "Whistling a fortune down the wind!"

"Legally mine, perhaps," Charmian had answered. "Rightfully, no. I have no shadow of a claim to Lord Medhurst's money. It was settled upon Mama for the maintenance of his child. I wonder if he even knows that the child did not survive infancy."

Susan had looked startled. "Maybe he doesn't, at that," she had admitted uneasily. "It was agreed between the four of them that there was to be no letters nor messages except just the one to the lawyer's to tell of Miss Melanie's birth. But I still hold that the money was given to Miss Bel to make up for the wrong that was done her, and that it was hers to spend or to give as she thought fit," she ended defiantly.

Charmian did not take up the argument. "I shall not be penniless, you know. There is this house and the money from the sale of the Virginia farm. We shall do very nicely so long as we hold household. And I have been well taught—at Lord Medhurst's expense. Perhaps I could obtain a post as a governess in a school. I believe Miss Somersby would recommend me for *that*, though I don't suppose a private family would employ me without an impeccable pedigree to vouch for my gentility."

Susan had snorted. "More fools they! A body has only to look at you to know you're a thoroughbred. And setting aside the fine bones of you and the way you carry yourself, who but the quality would have such mad-brained notions about money and honourable dealing!"

And here, now, came Susan herself, to warn that lunch was almost ready. "As nice a rabbit pie as you could wish, and a curd pudding to follow. So just you leave writing letters and don't let it spoil. Maybe we'll be down to bread and dripping before long, seeing as we've got such hoity-toity ideas, so best make the most of good hot food while you've got the chance," she ended gloomily.

However she was considerably appeased by Charmian's patent appreciation of her culinary labours and very ready to listen and advise when the girl confided her difficulties with the all-important letter.

"I must have wasted a dozen sheets of paper, not to mention a whole morning I could have put to better use," said Charmian ruefully. "How would it be if I journeyed to Medhurst and sought an interview with his lordship? I expect he is already aware of Mama's death, since it was announced in the *Gazette*, but it is very difficult to explain my place in her affairs, especially if he doesn't know about the baby dying."

Susan frowned thoughtfully. "Like enough you'd find him at Medhurst," she agreed slowly. "Seems to live very retired these days. I've always kept my ears open for news of him. You couldn't help liking him, though I guess there was a soft streak in his make-up. By all accounts he never made much of his life after he left Miss Bel. Got a name for playing high and taking reckless chances. But the last I heard he'd given up the Town house, so maybe he's learned sense at last or maybe he's purse-pinched. His lady's very well liked."

Susan had easily come to love the forlorn waif that chance had sent into Bel Tracy's lonely life, first from natural compassion, then out of gratitude that the child should have restored Miss Bel to something of her former self. The carefree, laughing girl who had grown up on the Virginia farm was gone forever, but at least she was human and alive again. She tended the baby Charmian quite devotedly, smiled proudly over her progress and chuckled at her mischief. And if she was a mite tetchy at times, well that was nothing to be wondered at, with all she had suffered.

Just when her own love for the girl had become fiercely, maternally protective, Susan herself could not have told you. Perhaps when she saw her so put upon by Miss Bel during her illness. For her own part, Susan had accepted the invalid's whims and pettishness with stolid good humour, but it was hard to see the young thing so hurt and sore, seeking some fault in herself that might be mended by patient application. And there could be no gainsaying that where Miss Charmian was concerned there were times when the mistress could be downright spiteful. Never come to terms with her for not being Miss Melanie, surmised Susan shrewdly, and swallowed her own anger in pity for Miss Bel's sad case, contenting herself with shielding the girl from injustice whenever she could.

She had woven dreams, too, about a future in which Miss Charmian would emerge from her present rustic seclusion and take her place in the world of fashion. Marriage would naturally follow, and then there would be babies for Susan to cosset and cuddle. But these dreams had lost all claim to practicability when Miss Charmian had decided to renounce her inheritance. Susan was well aware that a substantial portion would be needed to get a young lady of unknown parentage creditably married. Some new scheme must be devised, and it seemed to Susan that a meeting between her young mistress and Mr. Philip—Viscount Medhurst she must remember to call him—could be very helpful.

So she listened respectfully to Charmian's plans and hopes, even accepting the suggestion that Lord Medhurst, if he proved friendly and approachable,

Mira Stables

might be able to advise on the best way of tracing the girl's family.

"Not that I can see much chance of success," she warned, "not after all this time. But he could advise you about your future. And if you're really set on being a governess," she added cunningly, "maybe her ladyship could help you, too. It would be a great thing for you if she was to take a liking to you." And her natural optimism began to picture the endless possibilities of such a happy outcome, so that she became more and more enamoured of the scheme.

Charmian, who felt that she was perfectly competent to decide her own future, had no particular desire to seek the liking, far less the patronage of the Medhursts. But Susan's approval of the projected journey would make life more comfortable so she said nothing to depress her well-wisher's enthusiasm.

As it was there was heated argument over travelling arrangements, Susan holding to it that a hired chaise and a respectable abigail to play propriety were essential to the travels of a young lady with any claims to gentility, Charmian retorting that *she* had no such claims and that it was quite customary for governesses to travel unaccompanied by stage coach. Eventually they compromised. The cost of making the whole journey by chaise was too high for a slender purse, but Charmian consented to hire the chaise from the Saracen's Head for the first stage. It was not the most dashing of vehicles but it would serve to take her as far as Bolney, where she could board the London Mail. Susan felt that she could rely on the driver, old Jerry Bolt, to see his young passenger safely embarked, and surely no harm could come to her in the Mail? It might be a little awkward when she reached Medhurst. Never having visited his lordship's home, Susan had no idea how far it was from the posting house. It was all very well for Miss Charmian to declare that she was perfectly capable of hiring a vehicle to take her the rest of the way. Susan had a better idea. A letter to Mr. Philip, advising him of the girl's coming would ensure that she would be met and suitably attended. Miss Charmian need know nothing about it and Susan would cheerfully endure the resultant scolding at some future date, since the arrangement would relieve her mind of present care.

There was no difficulty about obtaining tickets. Few people would choose to travel in February if they could avoid it, but Charmian felt that enough time had been wasted already. There had been endless delays while the lawyers sorted out the details of Mama's affairs, ensuring that Lord Medhurst's settlement was left untouched while all dues and bequests were met out of the residue of the estate. Now she wanted only to be done with the whole business and to set about re-shaping her life. Even the half-formed notion of asking his lordship's help in tracing her family had been abandoned. Why should he put himself to so much pains? She had no claim on him—and to be asking a favour in the next breath when she had just put him under some obligation to her was not at all to her fastidious liking.

She set out on her journey with mixed feelings. A difficult interview lay ahead of her. But it *was* several hours ahead. Meanwhile she could yield to the excitement of travel; of travel even in February. When one is twenty-two or thereabouts and has been kept secluded all one's days, there is something exhilarating in the prospect of wider horizons, even if they are abounded by the windows of a shabby chaise. She had rarely travelled further afield than to East Bourne where she had gone to school. Mama had never permitted her to accept holiday invitations from her friends, explaining that she was not in a position to return such hospitality. She still exchanged letters with one or two of those friends, though less frequently as the years went by, and the letters brought her a tantalising glimpse of life in the world of fashion. Now, in a humble way, she would see for herself. Small wonder that her heart beat faster as she stepped up into the chaise that was to carry her to adventure.

Even as it drew slowly away and she waved her farewell to Susan, she smiled at so ridiculous a notion. Surely she was old enough now to distinguish between the probable and the highly unlikely. The only adventure she was likely to encounter was some small travelling mishap. The undistinguished vehicle was likely to attract the attention of that veritable figure of romance, the highwayman. And the commonsensical side of her nature strongly suspected that such gentry were not as romantic as the story books made out. She would very much dislike surrendering her purse of carefully counted guineas to such a one, be he never so handsome and gallant. She patted it reassuringly, where it lay snug in the pocket of her travelling mantle, and devoted her attention to a sodden grey landscape.

What she had not allowed for was the condition of the roads after a week of February's characteristic weather. The wayside ditches were a-brim, and a stream so insignificant as to be nameless had quietly undermined a low bridge which carried the road across a marshy stretch. Fortunately her driver was proceeding with extreme care, but as the carriage drew on to the weakened structure there was a low rumble, the surface of the bridge shuddered and cracked, and the road slowly sudsided, taking the rear wheels of the chaise with it.

By some lucky chance there was little damage. One of the horses had strained a fetlock, but after careful examination Jerry ventured to hope that there was no other injury. The ancient chaise had acquired a few more dents and scratches and one of the doors had been wrenched open so violently that it now refused to close until he secured it with a length of twine. The old man himself had managed to cling to his lofty perch though he grumbled that he must have looked uncommon foolish with his legs kicking in the air. Charmian, who had been toppled from her seat, was shaken but unhurt. She managed to scramble out in a rather undignified fashion, landing on hands and knees in the mud, and consulted with Jerry as to what was best to be done. It was clearly beyond the strength of the one sound horse to pull them out of their fix, but once again the luck was with them. The accident had occurred within easy reach of a small inn. One, moreover, well known to Jerry, who assured her that both help and horses would be forthcoming. In fact a kindly landlady insisted that Charmian drink hot coffee and helped her to sponge the worst of the mud from her skirts while the menfolk disappeared to the scene of the accident.

The rescue operation was not particularly complicated but it took up a good deal of time. There could be no thought, now, of catching the London Mail, and this was a serious reverse. An expensive ticket would be wasted, and more time lost. It might even be necessary to spend a night away from home. Jerry looked at her anxious face and said gruffly, "Don't you fret about the Mail, missy. No reason why I shouldn't drive you to Medhurst. Jake here has a good sound pair, fit for a fifteen mile stretch. Nor I don't mind leaving my cattle with him, he being wise-like with sick beasts. We'd need one change, maybe two, but I reckon we could reach Medhurst before the darkening. How would that be?"

It was the best she could hope for unless she was willing to concede defeat and go meekly home. And she was *not* willing. It would be to ruin her first real adventure. She closed her ears to a voice that murmured of finances stretched to the limit and accepted Jerry's suggestion. The landlady, by this time taking a motherly interest in Charmian's affairs, offered to send her son with a message to Susan, and the pair set off on the next stage of their journey.

Even Charmian secretly admitted that it soon became tedious. Besides she was steadily getting hungrier. Excitement had prevented her from eating very much breakfast; economic necessity prevented her from repairing the omission. She announced languidly that travelling always made her queasy; that she could not fancy anything. And watched with secret envy while Jerry consumed a couple of meat pasties and half a dozen sausages during the first change. The old man complained bitterly that this new pair were slugs. Certainly progress was very slow and it was mid afternoon before they reached Merton. Upon enquiry Jerry was told that Medhurst was scarcely a mile away, so they decided that they need not change horses again for so short a distance.

With the end of the journey in sight, something of Charmian's initial nervousness returned. Her head was aching and she felt slightly sick, partly from hunger and partly from the shock of the accident. To these discomforts was added the knowledge that daylight was already fading and that there were very few coins left in her purse. Scarcely enough to pay for a night's lodging, even in the humblest of hostelries, and certainly not enough to cover the cost of her return journey. It had been foolish to set out so ill provided but she had been nervous about carrying a larger sum. She could see no way out of the difficulty except the distasteful one of borrowing from Lord Medhurst. What a figure she would cut, she thought crossly, coming to make what now struck her as a rather theatrical offer of renouncing a comfortable competence and ending up by having to request a temporary loan! A woman of principle should be able to ignore such minor matters but Charmian was tired and hungry and nervous, and still young enough to dread ridicule. She sat very erect in her dilapidated chariot and tried to concentrate her thoughts on the passing scene.

It was scarcely calculated to evoke admiration. They came to a pair of handsome gates which stood hospitably open, but the lodge which guarded them was shuttered and silent with the derelict air bestowed by shabby paintwork and dirty windows, and the drive itself was ill-kept. It seemed, too, that someone had been felling timber. Several raw stumps marked the scene of the crime, for crime it was, thought Charmian indignantly, to fell trees that must have been eighty years and more a-growing. She could only conclude that Lord Medhurst must be hard pushed indeed if he was reduced to such desperate measures. Insensibly comforted by the thoughts that her offer might be more timely than she had dreamed possible, she forgot her anxieties and peered eagerly ahead for the first sight of the house.

Her knowledge of the ways of the great world was elementary. She had visited Brighthelmstone and seen the houses of the wealthy patrons and the Prince Regent's beloved Pavilion which Mr. Nash was going to turn into an oriental fairy palace, and she had seen pictures of Woburn. She supposed that the home of a Viscount would be of a similarly imposing character, and had secretly resolved that she would not permit herself to be over-awed. So she was not prepared for an unpretentious but charming house, low and sprawling, an old Elizabethan manor, built in mellow rosy brick and partly timbered. Its tall chimneys and quaint gables gave it a homely, welcoming air. Some attempt had been made to modernise it, perhaps in the reign of Queen Anne, but there was certainly no suggestion of cold Palladian magnificence. It was the kind of house that one would love and cosset with gifts to enhance its attractions, though at the moment it looked a little lonely and desolate. Perhaps that was the effect of the grey February light, or the fact that as yet the lamps were not lit. There should have been a flood of golden light glowing from the ancient casements to underline the note of welcome. But in summer, with beds and borders gay with flowers, it would be delightful.

Nevertheless it was with some trepidation that Charmian trod up the worn semi-circular steps that led to the front door and gave the bell-pull a tentative tug. It was shockingly late to be paying a call but there was no help for it. And at the very last moment, just as she heard footsteps approaching the venerable oaken door, she wondered if she should have furnished herself with visiting cards. She had never possessed anything of the kind, but it meant that she was faced with the difficulty of announcing herself and explaining her errand to a strange and possibly intimidating butler.

But the gentleman who opened the door was certainly not a butler, though his appearance was sufficiently intimidating. Of powerful build and well above average height, he showed to advantage in the casual country rig of buckskins and well-worn jacket. Charmian had barely time to decide that this could not possibly be Lord Medhurst. Setting aside the fact that a peer of the realm would hardly be answering his own front door bell, this man was much too young.

Whoever he was, he noted her hesitant air with an impatient eye and said curtly, "Yes?"

It was scarcely an encouraging welcome but in fact it served better than a more courteous address since Charmian was stung to indignation and forgot her diffidence.

"Good afternoon, sir," she said stiffly, and even in her own ears she sounded like a reproving governess. "My name is Tracy, and I wish to see Lord Medhurst.'"

This information was received with a slight nod of comprehension and a marked lack of enthusiasm.

"Ah, yes," he said coolly. "The young lady who was to have arrived by the Mail. I believe that Mama directed one of the servants to meet you, but since you did not arrive she concluded that you must have changed your mind. And I regret that you have had your journey in vain. Lord Medhurst is not able to receive you."

"Not able to receive me? But I *must* see him. My business is of some importance." His remarks about the Mail were a mystery, since she knew nothing of Susan's well-intentioned meddling, but that was unimportant. "I have undertaken an inconvenience to accomplish it," she pointed out.

"It would have been wiser to write to his lordship first, requesting an interview," suggested the gentleman suavely. "You would have been spared a deal of trouble and expense, since you would have been informed that his health does not permit of visitors."

The disappointment was severe, but it was short-lived. A gentle cough drew Charmian's gaze to the great staircase, down which came a dignified black-clad figure—the butler, much as she had imagined him, save for the benevolence of his expression, a pleasant-faced abigail following in his wake.

"Her ladyship asked me to say, sir, that if it is the young lady who was expected by the Mail, perhaps she will be good enough to wait. His lordship has just roused and she cannot leave him at the moment, but she is most anxious to speak with Miss Tracy and begs her to forgive the seeming discourtesy of her welcome. Here is Nan to wait on her if she wishes to freshen up after her journey, and tea and cakes will be sent up to the parlour. Milady hoped that you would be at liberty, sir, to see to the visitor's entertainment."

There was a glint of humorous understanding in the old man's eyes. Charmian badly wanted to laugh. Her opponent was completely taken at fault, his discomfiture slightly ludicrous.

He made a swift recovery. "Certainly. It shall be as Mama wishes," he bowed gravely, the faintest possible stress on 'Mama'. "And Noakes will see to it that your coachman and horses are also suitably refreshed," he added, eyeing the dejected looking pair of commoners who stood with heads a-droop under old Jerry's soothing hands.

She flushed with annoyance. That should have been her first concern of course. But in her high-strung state and her unfamiliarity with travel she had forgotten. She had forgotten, too, the appearance that she must present, her mantle mud-stained, her hands and hair grubby and untidy. Nor did that pitiful equipage do anything for her consequence. For a moment she saw it through the eyes of a stranger—the shabby paintwork, the cracked leather, the overworked job horses. Even Jerry, in his old-fashioned driving coat, a comforter tucked into the neck because he was subject to chest colds, his square-toed buckled shoes and ancient cocked hat, was a figure of fun. Yet a figure so homely and familiar to Charmian that she had never thought how comical he looked. And any way, she thought fiercely, he was worth a dozen of this smug, top-lofty creature who kept a chilled, weary girl standing on his doorstep while he debated whether or not to admit her. But for that one brief moment she wished passionately that she might have swept up to his door in a coach and six, an impressive crest emblazoned on the gleaming panels, a liveried footman to ring the bell for her and an attentive abigail hovering protectively in her wake. Then she smiled at her own folly and thanked Noakes politely, asking that Jerry might have something hot to drink since his chest was weak and the day a raw one, and turned thankfully to the waiting Nan.

THREE

IT WAS SURPRISING HOW MUCH BETTER
one felt when one was clean and tidy. Nan had
conducted her to a comfortable bed-chamber and
brought warm water and fine soap for her toilet. She
had suggested that the mud-stained mantle should
be laid aside, asked if she might try her skill at removing the marks, and listened with rapt attention
to miss's account of the mishap which had caused
them. Soothed and encouraged by this treatment—
for Nan, except for her more refined speech, seemed
very much like Susan—it was a more poised and
confident Miss Tracy who was presently ushered into
the parlour. Hot tea and the delicious wafers and
little cakes that were offered for her delectation
added still more to her sense of well-being. She
began to look about her, interested in her surroundings, and since her companion's remarks were limited to the necessary courtesies of hospitality she
was able to form a clear impression of a comfortable

well-used room, perhaps a trifle shabby as to carpet and curtains but charmingly furnished and beautifully kept. Had she been alone she would have enjoyed browsing along the well filled bookshelves and examining the ornaments and curios that filled the various cabinets. As matters stood, she felt that she must make some effort at fulfilling her social obligations.

She was quite unaccustomed to society, especially masculine society, but she had been taught that a lady must bear her share of the conversational exchange, and she felt that the periodical utterance of 'Yes please,' and 'Thank you, they are quite delicious,' was hardly adequate to this purpose. She decided upon a civil enquiry about Lord Medhurst's health, expressing the hope that his indisposition was of a passing nature and not unduly painful.

The remark met with no response. She glanced up in some surprise, meeting her host's gaze fully and shrinking disconcerted from the savage blue glare.

"Do you think to gull me with this display of filial concern?" he said softly. "I am happy to assure you, ma'am, that Papa's state gives no cause for present anxiety. The physician encourages us to hope that he may live for several years and that his command of his faculties will gradually improve. A sad disappointment for you, I fear. There are no more pickings to be hoped for at the moment."

Sick dismay choked her. Though she did not

fully grasp his meaning, there could be no mistaking the dislike, even contempt, in voice and expression.

She sprang to her feet. "I d-don't know what you mean," she began, half stammering in her distress, and then, indignation at the unwarranted attack driving out all other considerations, she stopped short, folding her pretty lips together resolutely. For a moment she stood so, arranging her thoughts carefully. Then she said with quiet dignity, "My business with Lord Medhurst is private and I have no intention of discussing it with you. But I can assure you that the last thought in my head when I planned this visit was to seek any kind of financial support from him."

She was really quite a taking little thing, decided Randolph Heriot critically, with the sparkle of anger in the big brown eyes and the colour that it had lent to her cheeks. Not in the least like Papa, but quite a presentable half-sister. She might even be as honest as she sounded. Mama was always scolding him for hasty judgements and intolerance. Perhaps he had made a mistake in this case. He said curiously, "Then why the parade of poverty? The talk of travelling by the Mail? The dilapidated chaise and the broken-down retainer?"

There was no doubt about the colour in her cheeks now. They were crimson with fury and wrath had evidently deprived her of speech. He went on smoothly, "I naturally assumed that you had dissipated your inheritance. That particular foible

41

is in your blood, as I have good cause to know. Did you not come to cast yourself upon Papa's generosity? I daresay he would have welcomed you gladly had he been in control of his own affairs. But fortunately for Mama, I am in the driving seat now, and I am not near so easy to cozen. I would not see you starve—so far I would subscribe to the claims of kinship—but I would certainly not support you in luxurious idleness. So if you have any pretty dreams of that nature, my girl, dismiss them. If you wish to stay, you'll have to make yourself useful."

But Charmian had recovered from her stunned amazement. "Pray do not strain your charitable instincts on my behalf, sir," she told him sweetly. "I would sooner starve in the gutter than turn to *you* for support. Fortunately I am not yet reduced to such straits. As for claiming kinship, I would rather claim it with that broken-down retainer whom you describe so scathingly, for he is more of the true gentleman than *you* have shown yourself." And then, coming down from this lofty attitude with a bump, she went on fiercely, "You are the rudest, horridest wretch that it has ever been my misfortune to meet, and I can only trust that our acquaintance will be of the briefest," with which she turned her back on him, walking across to the window with something perilously close to a flounce and staring out determinedly into the darkening evening in an effort to force back the ridiculous tears. For he would never believe that they were tears of sheer rage.

His voice sounded quite different this time, though the amusement in the softened tones was almost as infuriating as his earlier base assumptions. "Come down from the boughs, little sister. I will apologise for the whole. I am everything that you say, but, unlike you, I begin to believe that there may be some amusement to be got, after all, from our relationship. Now do, pray, sit down and drink your tea, or I shall be in disgrace with Mama for not looking after you properly."

It was the kind of apology with which one soothes a ruffled child but she guessed that it probably represented a handsome concession on his part. She turned slowly from the window, just as a third voice said gently, "Quarrelling already, children? I was for ever being told that I was blessed in having only the one son; that families squabbled incessantly, cutting up all one's peace. But half an hour seems to be very short acquaintance for the two of you to have come to cuffs. What has this wicked son of mine been saying to distress you, my dear?"

Had they been indeed the rebellious youngsters of her suggestion, the pair could hardly have looked more guilty. Their glances met. Charmian recognised triumphantly that there was open appeal in Mr. Heriot's blue eyes and promptly decided that he should see how a lady could behave.

"Why, nothing," she smiled pleasantly, as she curtsied to the little lady who had come in so quietly. "He has looked after me very well. We were just discussing the useful, as opposed to the ornamental qualities of my sex." And that at least bore some resemblance to the truth and should put a stop to further enquiry, she thought, and wondered if it was gratitude that lent such a pleasant aspect to Mr. Heriot's rather harsh featured countenance.

There was no time to dwell on this pleasing possibility for she must pay attention to a flow of enquiry as to her recent journey and present comfort and explain how it was that she had not arrived by the Mail. The mystery of Susan's letter was explained and Lady Medhurst chuckled sympathetically over the managing ways of old family servants.

"Was she your nurse? And cannot yet believe that you are out of leading strings?"

Charmian smiled back. "My nurse, and Mama's. And showed great devotion in consenting to come to England with her, since she is a very bad traveller. So one cannot scold her for her interfering ways. And it was not her fault that she misled you."

Then she must tell all about the accident and be praised and exclaimed over as though she had behaved like a heroine. It was absorbing and even exciting to be talking so easily to a real live Viscountess, she thought childishly. Though it was difficult to remember that this forthright, friendly little lady was of such exalted rank. She would dearly have loved to linger, savouring the experience to the full and storing it all in her memory for later relation to Susan. But other matters were pressing on her mind, and the entry of Noakes to light the candles recalled her to the every day world. She watched the old man carrying his taper from one candleholder to the next in stately fashion and wished that Mr. Heriot would take his departure that she could explain her difficulties to his mother —so much the more approachable. Why could he not make the very credible excuse of changing his dress for dinner, and take himself off. Surely he did not dine in riding clothes?

Alas! The gentleman seemed wholly unaware of the passage of time and the embarrassment created by his presence. He stretched long legs luxuriously towards the blazing logs and commented affably on the pleasant contrast between the February murk outside and the comfort of the parlour. There was no help for it. Charmian forced a little laugh and assumed a playfulness she was far from feeling.

"It is not kind in you, sir, to draw my attention to that contrast, since I must so soon forsake your hospitable hearth for the horrid murk. Already I have lingered too long. If you would be so kind as to have my carriage brought round"—and broke off short, colouring furiously at the high-sounding words, innocently though she had spoken them. She tried again. "And perhaps you could tell me"—she turned to Lady Medhurst—"when it will be possible for his lordship to receive me? As I explained to your son, it was a business matter that brought me here, and not one that I wished to broach to a lawyer since it concerned myself as well as his lordship."

Lady Medhurst looked puzzled and distressed, Mr. Heriot half sardonic, half quizzical, as though amused by the intruder's persistence. Mother and son exchanged glances, but it was Mr. Heriot who spoke, though this time his rebuff was more gently given, perhaps in deference to his mother's presence.

"Did I not make myself clear? I am sorry. My father never fully recovered from the wounds that he received during the American campaign. A few months ago he was taken ill quite suddenly. The physician called it a seizure, though precisely what that meant he did not specify. At any rate Papa was unable to speak clearly or get about without assistance, and his understanding was clouded. He is now very much improved, but it will probably be months"—he hesitated slightly, glancing at his mother—"if ever, before he can transact business again. Though we have good hopes," he ended cheerfully, "that he will continue to improve."

Lady Medhurst took pity on Charmian's obvious dismay. "Can we not forget business matters, for tonight at least? You are tired out, child. In any case I could not dream of permitting you to leave at this late hour. There is only one inn that you could reach before nightfall and it is quite unsuitable for a young lady. You shall stay with us tonight, which will be much more comfortable, and will give you time to think over your business with my husband in the light of the new circumstances. I am sure that Rolf will be very happy to advise you to the best of his ability if you wish it. For myself, I fear I have no head for business. But I do know how to make a tired girl comfortable," she nodded happily. "Rolf— you are very much in the way. Miss Tracy and I will do better on our own."

Mr. Heriot departed so meekly that Charmian would scarcely have recognised the abrupt, curt-spoken gentleman of her first impression. Plainly he adored his mother, and Charmian did not wonder at it. If his seeming harshness was designed to protect her from the encroachments of those who would impose on her generosity, then it was understandable and probably necessary, though it was not very flattering that he should, on sight, have placed *her* in this undesirable category. However, in the relief of his departure she found that she could forgive him.

"Now, my dear," said the Viscountess briskly. "Don't imagine that you are putting upon my hospitality. If only you could know what a delight it is to have another woman to talk to when one lives so isolated and largely confined to the house! And don't worry about your man or the horses. There is room and to spare in both stables and quarters since we put down the second carriage. Did you bring a portmanteau? No? Oh dear! What a pity.

We are near enough of a size that I can lend you all you need for the night, but you are so pretty that I would dearly have loved to see you in evening dress."

This flood of kindly suggestions was very pleasant but Charmian knew that she must not allow herself to be swept away. She was quite willing to defer the business of her visit until next day, but one fact at least must be revealed before she could avail herself of the hospitality so freely offered. It was with a bluntness worthy of Mr. Heriot himself that she said, "Your ladyship is very kind to a stranger. But I think that perhaps your kindness is partly dictated by the belief that I am Lord Medhurst's daughter. And I am not."

There! It was out. And Lady Medhurst did not immediately draw herself up in anger that she had been so deceived. She just looked puzzled and said, "But you are Miss Tracy, are you not? The letter came from Wivelsfield which is where—And it certainly said that Miss Tracy planned to travel by today's Mail."

Charmian nodded. "Oh, yes. I am the person you were expecting, and I have always gone by the name of Tracy—Mama's name. But she was not my true mother any more than Lord Medhurst was my father. Mama—adopted me, I suppose I might say —after her own baby died. You did not know of its death? I have only recently learned the truth myself. It is a long story and I will not weary you with the details. But I cannot accept your kindness without explaining that I am a nameless waif. Not even Mama knew who my parents were."

Lady Medhurst smiled a little at the determination in the proud little face. "I believe you half expect me to turn you away from my doors forthwith," she said mildly. "A great many persons, my dear, know little or nothing of their parentage, and some, I fear, have parents whom they would very much like to disown. Your friends will value you for your loveable qualities, not for your lineage. I can see that your situation distresses you, so for your sake I will hope that you may be able to discover the truth. It is possible, you know, that your Mama did not try very hard to do so, for fear that she might be obliged to give you up to relatives with a better claim."

It was exactly the right touch. Charmian's fierce young dignity melted in face of this matter-of-fact approach. She even managed a rather shaky chuckle. "I'm sorry, ma'am. I didn't mean to enact you a Cheltenham tragedy. It is just that I have not yet grown accustomed. It is a very—a very lowering feeling, not to belong anywhere. And to make matters worse, I have managed today's business so ill and am sadly set down in my self esteem. If you *had* chosen to turn me away, I should then have had to fling myself upon your charity. I did not allow for delays and changes of plan. The funds I brought are insufficient to cover a night's lodging and the expense of my return, and I am not yet familiar with the business of drawing money from the bank. It is not the kind of tale that one can tell with pride. And in my own defence I can only plead that my intentions were honourable."

She was half laughing at her own ineptitude, but the brown eyes were suspiciously bright. Lady Medhurst said slowly, "And your intention was—no, do not tell me—to inform my husband that you were not his child and to ask if you might rightfully keep the money that he settled on your mother."

The tear-bright eyes flew wide and Charmian gave a little startled gasp. "How could you guess?" she demanded, awed. "Though not precisely to *ask* about the money, which of course I cannot keep, so much as to arrange about its repayment."

Lady Medhurst tactfully ignored this. "Easy enough to guess," she smiled, and patted the girl's cheek. "Half an hour of your society and your own account of your affairs, and it was not difficult to predict how you would react. But we decided that business should wait until tomorrow. And I must tell Nan about having a room got ready for you. Meanwhile let us look through my wardrobe and see if there is anything that you could possibly wear tonight."

But the search for an evening gown proved fruitless. The capacious presses could supply nightrobe and dressing gown, for it would not matter that they were too full or too long; but milady's dresses hung in comical folds on Charmian's slight body. "Sparrow bones," she told her guest in playful exasperation. "And I had thought the brown lutestring was just the thing, since it is too tight for me. A pity, for the colour suits you beautifully."

Charmian smiled at her. There is nothing quite like trying on someone else's clothes for breaking down barriers of formality, and by this time the two were on the easiest terms. "It looks as though my own green will have to suffice," she agreed. "I hope it will not distress Mr. Heriot too much, to be obliged to sit down to dinner with me in a crumpled gown."

Lady Medhurst's eyes narrowed in amusement. "So there is something of the minx in you after all," she said. "And my poor Rolf *did* set up your prickles. You must forgive him. He is not very adroit with females, having been too preoccupied with premature responsibility to have time for the playful flirtations that a young man normally enjoys. I daresay he suspected you of having designs on his father's purse and will be sadly cast down to discover how far he misjudged the situation. By the way, have I your permission to tell him that you are *not* his half sister? He will obviously have to know sooner or later."

Charmian agreed, whereupon the little lady was off on another tack. "My dear! I have just remembered another dress. Would you object to its being slightly démodé? It is one that I laid aside in a fit of foolish sentiment because I had a fondness for it, and it is precisely the same shade of bronze-brown as the lutestring."

She was off across the room to what had once been a powdering closet. Having outlived this use, it had been shelved out to form a repository for a varied collection of domestic treasures too precious for disposal. Charmian caught a fleeting glimpse of a child's hobby-horse and a pair of baby's shoes set side by side on a shelf before her hostess hurried back, clutching a rather dusty band-box.

"It is impossible to keep a house of this size in good order with so few servants," she said apologetically, blowing dust off the lid, "yet it would be foolishly extravagant to engage more when we live so quietly."

She lifted out the dress carefully and shook out its folds. "There would be time for one of the maids to press it for you, if you decide to wear it," she suggested, and looked hopefully at her guest.

Charmian's first reaction was dismay. The dress must be all of thirty years old. The bodice was cut so low as to make her blush. The skirt was voluminous, obviously designed to wear over a hoop. To be sure the fabric was finer than anything she had ever seen, a thick, supple taffeta that gleamed bronze and gold, with a foam of exquisite, creamy lace to form the underdress and the ruffles that cascaded from elbow to wrist. But no modern miss would choose to be seen in so antiquated a garment. Better by far her own plain gown, however unsuited to the dinner table.

And then she saw the dreamy half-smile on her hostess's face as she smoothed the rich breadths of silk with gentle fingers. There was nothing amiss in *her* eyes. One could only hope that the gown would not fit—and regret that it would be improper to pray about so trivial a matter.

Lady Medhurst, excited as a child, pulled out the hooped petticoat, exclaiming how fortunate it was that she had not thrown it away, and laced her into the tight bodice.

It fitted as though it had been made for her.

"There!" exclaimed its owner delightedly. "I knew it! Nothing could be better. And it will give me such pleasure to see you wear it."

After that, of course, one could not possibly decline. She did not venture tentatively to suggest that the décolletage was lower than she was accustomed to wearing, but it seemed that there was a fichu of lace that could be worn about the neck and shoulders.

"Though it seems a pity, with your skin so perfect," sighed the Viscountess, "but perhaps for a quiet dinner at home——"

Eyeing herself in the mirror, Charmian thought she looked more as though she was dressed for a masquerade or for private theatricals. And at the back of her mind was the thought of how Mr. Heriot would lift his brows and strive to mask his amusement. It was quite enough to make her put up her chin.

"That is exactly right," exclaimed her ladyship. "You must forget the modest bearing that you have been taught and hold your head high. And I will send Nan to dress your hair in an appropriate style."

She hurried off with the dress over her arm, leaving Charmian to smile ruefully over her dilemma. Well—at least she would be giving pleasure to her hostess, so why should she care for Mr. Heriot's opinion?

In the event there was no awkwardness at all, for she came down the stairs with Lady Medhurst, both of them laughing over her difficulties with the management of the hoop, to be greeted by an elegant gentleman formally arrayed in dark pantaloons and long-tailed coat and to find herself able to meet his gaze with calm nonchalance. Then Lady Medhurst was eagerly pouring out the history of the cherished gown and he was smiling down affectionately into her vivacious face and offering an arm to each lady to conduct them to the dining-room.

"—and do you not agree that she looks quite enchantingly in it? Fashions were much prettier when I was a girl," said his Mama happily.

"I count myself very fortunate that *both* my table companions look so delightfully," he returned, sketching a slight bow. "*Your* gown may be less elegant, Mama, but it is very becoming. And cer-

tainly you are in high bloom. I rather think that I
have Miss Tracy to thank for that. It seems that
her visit has already done you good." And for the
first time there was genuine warmth in the smile
that he bestowed on Charmian.

"Well, my dear," admitted his mother, "you are
the very best of sons, but you know that I have always wished for a daughter. Females are so much
more conversible. *You* cannot be expected to enter
into my enjoyment of domestic gossip any more
than I can share your enthusiasm for your breeding
flock. And while I am delighted to know of the
improvements that you are making at Rylands, you
will agree that one has to wait a very long time for
the results."

He grinned. "Agriculture is a slow business,
Mama. Nature refuses to be hurried. But I can
understand that Miss Tracy would share your more
feminine interest in cookery recipes and the latest
fashions."

Conversation continued on general and unimportant topics during the serving of the first course.
Charmian, at her first dinner party, was thankful
to find that the meal presented no awkward problems to the tyro. She was very hungry, and so was
especially thankful to enjoy dishes that were tempting and savoury but not entirely unrecognisable.
Relieved to find that the nobility dined so simply,
feeling herself quite sophisticated, she relaxed the

strict guard that she had been keeping on her behaviour and chattered away happily to her hostess. Mr. Heriot had little to do but put in the odd polite comment or question and watch the two absorbed faces. It was a pleasure to see his mother in such spirits, a laughing, sympathetic creature who might have queened it over a much more important gathering than this or—more to her taste, he thought tenderly—mothered a large family with a horde of grandchildren to tease and amuse her.

When the second course had been brought in the servants were dismissed. "Now we can talk freely," pronounced Lady Medhurst cheerfully. "I have already told Rolf that you are not his sister. Do pray tell us how it came about that Mrs. Tracy adopted you. I know you said that you would not weary us with all the details, but indeed I find it of absorbing interest. And Rolf may be able to offer some suggestion as to how you should set about tracing your family."

But when Charmian was done, Rolf shook his head dubiously. "It is a pity that so much time has been allowed to elapse," he said. "The description you give of your clothing obviously suggests some attempt at disguise. Either you had been stolen—though such a crime seems unlikely outside the pages of a melodrama—or stood in some kind of danger that necessitated your being secretly smuggled to safe keeping. From the few facts that we know—the strange dialect—the Cornish crew of the boat that put into Dover—and the fact that the events you have described took place when the Terror reigned in France, it occurs to me that you might be the child of a French royalist family, unable or unwilling to flee the country themselves but determined that their child should do so. You might have been sent to Brittany first—it was about the safest quarter of the country—and then, as the situation worsened, smuggled across to Cornwall. There was a good deal of illegal traffic between these two remote provinces throughout the war. But all of this is the merest surmise," he warned, realising that both ladies were hanging on his words and that Charmian's eyes looked huge as a young owlet's in her absorption. "The real story may be quite different. And although it is possible, now, to travel to France if you wished to make enquiries there, I believe that conditions are still chaotic, with all the emigrés flocking back to claim their properties and a number of sober citizens who have paid honestly enough for land that was seized by the Republican government, refusing to be dislodged. Moreover, if the tale were true, it would seem that your parents did not survive, for surely they would have tried to trace you before now."

Charmian looked rather cast down by these depressing suggestions. Lady Medhurst paid them small heed, being quite carried away by her son's display of imagination.

"It sounds just like a book," she murmured admiringly. "I shouldn't be surprised if that is exactly what *did* happen. Except for one thing. The name on the locket. Charmian. It is a very *English* name. Or that is how it strikes me."

Mr. Heriot shrugged, but humoured her by agreeing that possibly Charmian's mother had been an English girl who had married a Frenchman, at which she nodded contentedly, sat in silence for a few moments as though making sure that the story now hung together in a satisfactory fashion, and then gave a sudden exclamation of dismay and sprang up.

Charmian was about to rise too, but Lady Medhurst pressed her back into her chair. "No need for you to hurry, my dear," she explained. "But I was so interested that I forgot the time. I always sit with my husband after dinner. He is restless then and my company seems to soothe him. You will forgive my desertion. Rolf will look after you, and I will come down later to see that you have all that you need for the night."

With this she flitted out of the room. Rolf smiled at his companion. "You must not mind Mama," he said comfortably. "She has the happiest disposition and is now convinced that all is explained and that your troubles are as good as over."

"Mind?" returned Charmian impulsively. "I think she's a darling. No one could have been kinder to a stranger with no claim on her time or her interest."

His eyes warmed to approval. "Thank you. And I believe that you also deserve thanks on another head." And as she lifted her brows in enquiry, "I suspect that it was not quite to your taste to wear so—so striking a dress. No doubt you would have preferred your own more sober gown. You wore it to please Mama and you succeeded to admiration. I have not seen her look so young and carefree since Papa took ill, and I am very grateful, the more so since you had such a churlish reception at my hands. But it is neither gratitude nor contrition that prompts me to tell you that you present a very charming picture. I believe it is an object with young ladies to dress always in the current mode. If I were indeed your brother I would advise you to aim at being a little out of the common way. Not, perhaps," he smiled at her, "*quite* as markedly as you are tonight, for I suppose it would require a vast amount of self confidence to appear so in public. Which is a great pity, for your appearance could not fail to give pleasure to any person of taste or discrimination." He grinned suddenly. "Certainly to any gentleman," he amended.

Charmian blushed furiously. For one supposedly maladroit in female company, his compliments were amazingly fluent. She did not know quite how to deal with them, for they were the first she had ever received, unless one counted the time when the Rector had said that she was growing to be quite a pretty little puss, and then she had been no more than thirteen. But though she was embarrassed she was not displeased, for the frank praise sounded sincere and it was a comfort to know that she had not looked ridiculous in her borrowed plumage. She smiled at him shyly and then lowered her gaze, making haste to change the subject and quite unaware of the devastating effect of long, curling dark lashes as they brushed her smooth cheeks.

"The idea that I may be part French seems to me at least possible, sir. And though I may only discover that I am, in fact, an orphan, I would still like to make further enquiries. I do not relish the prospect of embarking upon what might well be a wild goose chase in foreign parts, but surely there are still a good many emigrés in this country—possibly in London. Do you think that enquiry among them might prove fruitful? Or there is the French Embassy. Though perhaps the Ambassador would be too grand and too busy to humble himself with such humble affairs."

It would be cruel to crush these innocent hopes entirely, though it was obvious that she had no notion of the vast field that would have to be searched.

"I expect he would concern himself in the kindliest way," he said pleasantly, "if we could prove that you were indeed of French parentage. But you must remember that that was the merest guesswork on my part with no real evidence to support it. And a prolonged search would be costly."

There was alarm and disappointment in the wide brown eyes for that. No doubt money was the problem in spite of the child's proud denials. To be sure the settlement had been generous enough, but that was years ago, and financial affairs left in feminine hands might well be in a shocking tangle by now. Perhaps that was what Miss Tracy—Charmian—pretty name—had wished to consult Papa about. He was prepared to acquit her of greed and self-seeking. Advice was a different matter. Any young girl left unprotected must long for the support of an older man in solving her difficulties. Possibly Mrs. Tracy had commended her to his father. He wondered if he might be permitted to act as a substitute. Meanwhile she was watching him with an expression of wistful hope in those lovely eyes, obviously expecting him to produce some brilliant scheme. It was a pity that common sense and practical possibility were more in his line than brilliance.

He played for time. "It is quite possible, you know, that all this while people have been searching for *you*. I doubt if your mother persevered in her enquiries for more than a month or so. She may not have wished to do so, once conscience was satisfied that she had done all that could reasonably be expected. Then, you know, your relatives might have been advertising for news of you, perhaps several months later—it *was* war time, remember—and this time it was your Mama's turn to miss the notices."

The suggestion took well. The anxious look vanished, the brown eyes were raised expectantly, trustfully to his.

"Then what would you suggest as my best course of action?"

It could do no harm, he felt, and it might do a great deal of good. "I believe," he pronounced firmly, "that your first move should be to take your place in a wider world. You have lived secluded all your life. How could anyone find you, hidden away in a tiny Sussex village, where chance alone had carried you? If you were to show yourself in fashionable circles there is a possibility that someone might recognise either a resemblance to your family or your unusual name."

She was aglow with eagerness. "What a perfectly splendid idea! Only"—hesitantly—"I am not quite sure how it could be managed. There is no one to sponsor me, and though I believe that one can find matrons of unimpeachable *ton* to do so for a suitable fee, I doubt if such a lady would accept a girl with so odd a story. Moreover, although Mama expressly forbade me to wear black for her, it is not yet four months since she died and I do not feel"——

Her hands went out in a gesture so expressive that for the first time he wondered if there might not in fact be some substance in the romantic tale of French blood that he had concocted. But he did not mean to encourage her in that belief. He said kindly, as though he had indeed been her elder brother, "Well that is where Mama can help us. What is more she will be delighted to give us her advice, and it will be a new interest for her."

FOUR

BUT ALTHOUGH LADY MEDHURST WEL-
comed the idea with enthusiasm, there were obvious
difficulties. Foremost among these was the question
of expense. It cost a great deal to launch a girl into
society, even when, as in Charmian's case, there
was no question of her being presented at Court.

Over the breakfast table the two ladies discussed
the extent of the wardrobe that she would require,
Mr. Heriot, having providentially—or prudently—
breakfasted early and gone off to exercise his mare,
tongues wagged happily and excitedly until the
question of cost arose.

"Oh dear!" said Charmian sadly.

There was a pensive silence. Then Lady Medhurst
said carefully, "You know there is not the least
need for you to be repaying the settlement money.
It was Mrs. Tracy's to use as she wished. If she had
been extravagant it might all have been spent years

ago. Do you think that you do right to run counter to her wishes on this head?"

But Charmian was not to be persuaded. Just because the temptation was so strong she was all the more anxious to have the matter settled before she could weaken. "By the same premises," she pointed out, "the money is now mine, to spend as I wish. And I wish to pay it back."

They seemed to have reached point non plus. Lady Medhurst had recourse to her never-failing solution. "We will ask Rolf," she said comfortably. "He will know how it can be managed. He always does."

Charmian had early discovered why Mr. Heriot found it necessary to use brusque methods of dealing with unknown visitors. At this moment she felt the dawn of sympathy for the unfortunate young man who was expected to solve all the problems created by his Mama's impulsive generosity. At least, she thought thankfully, *she* would not add to his difficulties.

Having relegated the financial side of the project to her son, Lady Medhurst had reverted to planning the absorbing details. "And no need to be searching around for a suitable lady to take you in charge, when my own sister would be happy to do so," she reflected aloud, just as Charmian emerged from her own reverie.

The girl was startled. "Your sister, ma'am?"

"My elder sister. The dearest creature, and so capable. I wonder that I did not think of it sooner."

It was clear that the business was already settled in Lady Medhurst's mind. She went on to describe her sister's house in Portland Place and her amiable husband who would not raise the least objection to his wife's accepting the charge of an unknown girl. Rather he would be delighted that Cecilia should be so well amused, for with both her daughters married and her son serving with the Army of Occupation she could have nothing in the world to do. Charmian felt slightly dazed. Apparently her hostess's generosity did not stop at the limits of her own capabilities. She was perfectly ready to pledge the services of others.

"It would be delightful if it could be arranged," she temporised politely. "If we could come to some arrangement so that I should not be a charge upon your sister, and if she should not think me too raw and ignorant, there is nothing I would like better. But, to be honest, I do not see how I can contrive to meet the expense of a season. Every time I think of it I remember some costly extra that would be essential. And my means are modest. Indeed, I had been considering the possibility of finding employment as a governess or companion, since I do not care to be idle. The days have seemed very long since Mama died."

Lady Medhurst thought this sober approach to life very poor-spirited. "You must do no such thing," she protested. "To be wasting your best years in attendance on some horrid old frump, or being teased to death by a parcel of impudent ill-bred brats! I never heard such nonsense. Rolf! Thank goodness you are returned. Do, pray, tell her that it is quite ridiculous."

Her son listened to her explanation with an air of mild amusement until she ended on an indignant, "And all she will say is that she is concerned about the expense. I cannot convince her that she is in no way bound to repay the money that was settled upon Mrs. Tracy."

She stopped short, an expression of dismay dawning, and said penitently, "I am so sorry, my dear. I forgot that Rolf did not know. Pray forgive me! But he must have found out eventually, you know, since he deals with all his Papa's business affairs. And at least, now, he can add his persuasions to mine."

But it seemed that her son was in no hurry to do so. He had pokered up a trifle at the disclosure of Charmian's intention, and had cast her a thoughtful, measuring look that seemed to question her sincerity. She met it calmly, discovering that she was actually thankful that matters had now been taken out of her hands.

"So that was your errand to my father," he said slowly. "And I——" He broke off. "I see. I hope you will allow me time to consider so delicate a business. You will understand that I have to put myself in my father's place—decide what he would have me do."

To the innocent Charmian it seemed a very reasonable request. "Though I hope you will decide as quickly as possible," she said shyly. "Susan will be wondering what has become of me. I ought to set forward on my return as soon as matters are agreed."

That provoked more protest from Lady Medhurst. She could not possibly part with her unexpected guest so soon. Surely Charmian could spare her a few days—those days that seemed so long. Jerry—was that his name?—could carry a letter to Susan to set her mind at rest, and a groom should go with him and bring back whatever Charmian needed, and Susan, too, if she so wished. Since Mr. Heriot endorsed this invitation, though more temperately, pointing out that it would allow him time to give serious consideration to the problem she had set him and stressing the pleasure that his mother would find in her society, Charmian allowed herself to be persuaded, and went off to the library to write her letter, secretly delighted at the prospect of prolonging this unusual treat. Lady Medhurst might believe that she was living very quietly, but to Charmian, Medhurst was a new world, exciting and intriguing. She could not help hoping that Mr. Heriot would not be too prompt in reaching his decision.

"Rolf!" said his mother reproachfully. "You are not really going to allow that child to beggar herself? I know that it is make and scrape with us, but surely things are not come to such a pass!"

He grinned at her good-humouredly. "Of course not. I'd as soon think of robbing a baby—or my sweet gullible Mama. I had to give myself time to concoct a tale that will fob her off. And it will have to be a good one. She may be green but she's not a ninny. And you, my darling Mama, had best set a guard on that indiscreet tongue of yours. Let her but get a hint that she is being tricked, and the game will be up."

His Mama earnestly promised amendment of her ways, and wished to know what tale he had in mind. He twinkled down at her, mischief in his eyes. "That I have not finally decided. Something abstruse to do with principal and interest accruing; which will take me some time to work out in order to achieve a plausible tale, and would certainly baffle a certain little Mama who cannot even balance the household books without cheating." And he hugged her so comprehensively that he lifted her right off her feet and refused to put her down until she vowed that she had forgiven him.

"By the way," he said suddenly. "I like your idea of sending her to Aunt Cecil. If she should chance to find herself a husband, all this fuss about her family will die a natural death. And if, by good fortune, her choice should fall upon a man of sub-stance, our responsibility will be at an end."

"So you *do* feel a certain responsibility for her?"

He shrugged. "Why—yes—to a certain degree. She seems to have played a daughter's part to that unfortunate woman. I would like to see her comfort-ably established."

His mother smiled. "Good. You do your part and I will do mine. I shall write to Cecilia this very day."

Charmian, meanwhile, had put aside care for the future and given herself up to enjoyment of her new surroundings. She could scarcely have had a more kindly introduction to the life of a large establish-ment. The servants were mostly middle aged or elderly, and devoted to their mistress. They were very willing to serve the young lady whose coming had so cheered her. And because Charmian was so naively interested in their various duties and re-sponsibilities and asked so many eager questions, she was soon on the friendliest terms with even such awe-inspiring personages as Noakes, and Butter-beck, Lord Medhurst's personal attendant. She ex-plored the unused reception rooms, where the furniture was all swathed in holland covers, and wondered what it would be like to attend a grand party there, with music and dancing. She browsed happily along the library shelves and longed to learn the histories of the curious objects that a much-travelled family had accumulated over the past two hundred years. She explored the gardens and stables, a little nervous of Mr. Heriot's spirited mare but making friends with an aged pony who was living out his old age in lazy comfort and with the fat cob that Lady Medhurst drove in the gig. And because, as she had truly said, she hated to be idle, she fell into the way of performing a number of small services for her hostess until that lady vowed that she did not know how she was to go on without her little friend when the time came for them to part.

Charmian, who had never been so petted and indulged in all her short life, smothered a twinge of conscience. For the moment she asked nothing better than to linger on at Medhurst, sunning herself in her ladyship's affection and soaking up the atmosphere of the old house as a thirsty plant soaks up summer showers. But she knew that she ought to press Mr. Heriot for his decision. It was no use pretending that the moment was not propitious. So busy and so contented as she was, it probably never would be. But she could not go on indefinitely sponging on Medhurst hospitality. For one thing, she had already seen evidence to suggest that the gold in the Medhurst coffers was at low ebb. There had been indications of this on that first afternoon but she had been too flustered to assess them properly. The mention of putting down a carriage, of not engaging extra servants, should have been enough to give her a hint. She was still too green to realise that the simplicity of the meals and the absence of all pomp were as much for economy's sake as because of a preference for informality, but even she was startled when Lady Medhurst let fall the information that the house and gardens, with a few acres of park land and grazing, was all that remained of the original estate.

"Not even the Home Farm?" she queried involuntarily, tactless in her shocked dismay.

But Lady Medhurst, as her son had said, had the happiest disposition. To be sure her expression as she shook her head was mildly regretful, but it quickly brightened again as she explained the fortunate chance that had permitted the tenants to buy the property when it came on the market. "For it would have been quite dreadful, you know, if they had been obliged to turn out. As it is, we go on very happily. Mrs. Maylie still supplies us with all the butter and cream and eggs that we need, and I'm sure I often forget that the land is no longer our own."

After that there could be no more putting off. But Mr. Heriot still proving elusive, it was, in fact, his volatile Mama who eventually provided the occasion, coming into the parlour before dinner with an open letter in her hand and announcing happily, "There! It is all arranged. I told you Cecilia would like it of all things. And you are to go to her as soon as you can conveniently do so, which will give you plenty of time for shopping before the season begins. Oh yes! She wishes to know whether you sing or play, and if you are well practised in the latest dances."

The latter part of this speech was, for the moment, lost on Charmian. "But I do not know—we did not decide——" And then, with dignity, "I regret that limited means will prevent me from taking advantage of your sister's kind invitation."

"Pray don't decline it out of hand," put in Mr. Heriot. "I have not forgotten your errand here, and I have been in consultation with my father's attorney who drew up the original Deed of Settlement. Perhaps you could spare time to discuss his view of your position later this evening. But meantime dinner is awaiting us and Mama will scold if we discuss such sordid things as securities and interest rates at table. Have you a head for business, Miss Tracy? Mama vows that balancing her household accounts is more than enough for any woman."

Miss Tracy then caused him some dismay by confessing that she had always found Mathematics fascinating. "I know it is supposed to be unfeminine," she admitted. "Miss Somersby was for ever telling me so. But sums are so neat and logical and satisfying." She smiled at Lady Medhurst. "Mama hated business, too. As soon as I left school the task of keeping the books and settling the bills was handed over to me."

This harmless reminiscence caused Mr. Heriot to go carefully through the tissue of half-truths with which he proposed, later, to regale the speaker. Provided that he stuck to generalities and used all the legal-sounding phrases that he could call to mind, he thought it was fairly water-tight.

Charmian, in her turn, wondered at his abstraction. Though their acquaintance was brief they had already fallen into a light, teasing camaraderie. He had answered her questions about the house and its contents, explaining things that puzzled her with a degree of patience that surprised his mother. Rolf had never been in the petticoat line. Some day, she vaguely realised, he would have to marry to ensure the succession. The subject was not openly discussed, but it was tacitly understood that he would have to look about him for an heiress. So his kindness to their little protegée was wholly admirable, she decided fondly. The two might indeed have been brother and sister, especially when they disagreed, for Charmian had never been taught to bow to the superiority of the masculine mind and so was apt to defend her views with a freedom and vigour that seemed downright revolutionary to the conventionally reared older woman. Certainly she showed no disposition to develop a tendre for Mr. Heriot, a danger which Lady Medhurst had anxiously considered when she saw the swift growth of intimacy between the pair. But then, despite her twenty-two years, she was very young, her manners as unaffected as those of a nice candid child. And the subjects on which they conversed and argued were unexceptionable—odd trophies from foreign parts, and the propriety of removing them from their native lands; old weapons—and the rights and wrongs of the causes in which they had been wielded; and, queerest of all, in Lady Medhurst's opinion, the theories put forward in a very learned and dry-as-dust book entitled 'The Wealth of Nations' which Charmian had discovered in the library. Lady Medhurst, who herself enjoyed reading poetry or a romantic novel when she had an hour to spare, thought it a very odd choice for a young girl. But at least there was nothing improper in it.

She withdrew, as usual, to her husband's apartments after dinner, leaving the two to their business talk and weaving hopeful plans for Charmian's future, since naturally she had no doubts about her son's persuasive abilities. Her son had no such illusions. This intelligent child would need careful handling if her suspicions were not to be aroused. With meticulous care he explained to her how the original capital had been invested in Consols. He spoke of interest rates, of premiums and discounts; of buying stock when the price was right, selling at a profit, investing in other sound concerns; and he resolutely refused to yield to the compassion that touched him at the sight of the smooth, childish brow furrowed in deep concentration.

When he felt that he had mystified her sufficiently, he broke off and awaited comment or question.

She said slowly, "I don't understand why the prices change so much. One would expect government stock to maintain a steady price, yet it seems that sometimes one may buy for as little as fifty pounds and then sell at a considerable profit a few weeks later."

He was considerably startled that she had understood even so much, and eyed her with increased respect. "It depends on the strength of government," he explained. "When things are going smoothly, the price of the stock goes up. In times of trouble—such as the late European struggle, for example—you may buy it very cheaply."

"But surely it is wrong to be making a profit out of one's country's difficulties?"

It was a simple view, a child's view, but privately he saluted her integrity.

"The government needs the money," he reminded her, "and must get it where it can." And then, on a lighter note, "And surely, to invest when things look blackest argues a sturdy patriotism that deserves some reward."

She flushed a little at the teasing she suspected. "I see," she said quietly. "Go on, please."

"As matters stand at the moment, just over half the original sum is still invested in the Funds. The remainder is divided between several commercial concerns. I will not take you into all the transactions—your lawyer holds the certificates—but having regard to the present unsettled trading conditions, your affairs are in a remarkably healthy state."

She said eagerly, "And you will arrange the repayment? Oh, thank you! Now I can be comfortable. You will put the arrangements in hand as quickly as possible? For the transfer of the money, you know."

He studied her curiously. No trace of disappointment, no hint of regret for the delights of a London season. The girl was true metal throughout. And even as he watched, the bright face clouded.

"I am sorry that your Mama was so definite in her letter to your Aunt. Do you think that she will have been put to any expense or inconvenience on my behalf?"

"Why, no," he told her, with an air of faint surprise. "But I trust that you do not mean to overset my mother's cherished plans. I know that the financial aspect was causing you some concern, but as I have just explained, there is not the least need. Surely even *your* scruples must be satisfied by repayment of the original sum involved. You could not expect my father to demand the profits as well! I can safely promise you that you will have more than sufficient to meet the expense of a London season.

As to the wisdom of spending it in that particular fashion, I cannot presume to judge."

She said doubtfully, "It is difficult. You see, apart from the possibility of stumbling across some clue to my identity, I want so very much to go. I daresay a gentleman might not understand a female's sentiments in such a case, but I should explain that until I came here I have been nowhere and have made no new acquaintance since I left school. And that is six years ago. Do you wonder that I am sorely tempted. If you can assure me that you think I do right, then certainly I shall not hesitate on the score of prudently hoarding my funds."

"Do you not feel that Mama would be a better arbiter?" he enquired, a little uneasy at the responsibility that she had thrust upon him. Mama, he knew, thought it probable that so charming and sweet-natured a girl would contract an eligible alliance without much difficulty if she was given a proper chance, but he was not qualified to judge.

Her sober expression vanished. She dimpled at him mischievously. "No," she told him. "She is much too tenderhearted to deny me the treat, since she would guess how much I desired it. I do not wish to cast aspersions on your disposition, sir, but I feel that I shall receive a less prejudiced verdict from you."

He grinned, flinging up one hand in the gesture of a fencer acknowledging a hit. With that mischievous glint in the big brown eyes, she was enchanting. Mama was undoubtedly right. A taking little thing.

"Then I think you would be well advised to accept Aunt Cecilia's offer, and shall look forward with confidence to hear that you have taken the 'ton' by storm."

FIVE

BY THE END OF THE WEEK EVERYTHING
was in train. The house at Wivelsfield was to be
closed. Susan had accepted an invitation to stay at
Medhurst, where, she didn't doubt, she said, but
what she could make herself useful in a dozen
different ways. She was too old to be jauntering off
to London and she had struck up a quaint, com-
bative association with Nan which seemed to afford
them both deep satisfaction. They had joined battle
over the merits of their respective countries, each
extolling such varying aspects as the magnificent
scenery, the excellence of regional dishes and the
infinite superiority of the moral code obtaining in
their respective homelands. A stranger, overhearing,
might have thought them embroiled in a fierce
quarrel, but they seemed to find their frequent
clashes exhilarating and each, in private, praised the
other to her mistress.

Mr. Heriot had so arranged matters financial as

to spare Charmian any embarrassment. That, at least, was how he put it to her. "You will not wish to be handing over sums of money to my Aunt as though she were some lodging house keeper. If I were you I would leave it to your lawyer to pay your dress bills and to settle such expenses as she incurs in your behalf. I daresay your personal income will be adequate for such small daily expenses as vails to servants who run errands for you and for cab fares should you ever chance to incur them."

They were small daily expenses that had never occurred to the inexperienced Charmian, and she would dearly have liked to seek further information; but pride forbade. She thanked him for his advice and never dreamed that he had deliberately introduced vails and cab fares as a red herring to distract her from enquiring too closely into the working of his first suggestion.

So the good understanding that had grown up between them remained unimpaired and it was a happy and excited girl that he handed up into the carriage that his Mama had lent for the journey, Charmian could not help smiling a little as she compared this vehicle with the chaise in which she had arrived. Its owner had apologised for its shabbiness, declaring that she really must see about having it re-lined if Rolf persisted in his refusal to let her buy a new one, but to Charmian it appeared both elegant and comfortable, while the crest on the door panel added a touch of fairy tale glamour to the occasion. She would have liked to share these reflections with her escort, but he had chosen to ride, and in the occasional glimpses that she had of him she had thought that he looked to be out of humour. She wondered if he was annoyed at being obliged to waste time on *her* insignificant affairs. His Mama had obliged him to defer his own departure from Medhurst so that he could escort her to Town. There were doubtless a dozen other things that he had rather be doing, and she was sure she did not blame him. She could perfectly well have managed without an escort for so short a journey but Lady Medhurst had insisted and Charmian had raised no protest, not because of any imagined danger from which Mr. Heriot might protect her, but because she longed for his support in the critical first encounter with his Aunt.

She had judged aright. Lady Cecilia was a little overpowering, smart London footmen positively intimidating. Life in Portland Place was obviously a good deal more formal than the easy way to which she had grown accustomed in friendly Medhurst. Dinner, with a bewildering array of unfamiliar dishes, was something of an ordeal, especially as she was subjected to a searching inquisition as to her tastes, talents, education and even her former school friends. It was a relief when her ladyship turned her attention to her nephew. But after one or two questions, obviously well-informed, about his progress at Ryelands, she came back to Charmian's affairs, and the girl was greatly heartened to hear Mr. Heriot give conditional acceptance to an invitation to attend the ball with which his Aunt proposed to launch her protegée into the 'ton'.

"I shall take her about to a few smaller parties first, so that she will meet people more intimately, and then when it comes to our own ball she will have plenty of partners to dance with and girls to gossip with. But I daresay she will be pleased to find one old friend among the crowd."

Lady Cecilia was quietly confident of success. This was a challenge wholly to her taste. The girl was an unknown, but she, who had studied the débutantes of the past twenty years, recognised the qualities that were needed. Properly dressed she would be ravishing. She had poise, good manners and good sense. And her complete lack of artifice made her unusual without being farouche. A little grooming, a hint or two about keeping a proper distance, and Lady Cecilia's world would *eat* the girl. A honey-fall indeed for a slightly bored matron of a sociable and managing disposition. Her ladyship sighed contentedly and was not in the least surprised that Rolf, dyed-in-the-wool bachelor that he was (and she spared an amused thought for the aptness of the description, since he seemed wholly preoccupied with his wretched sheep) admitted that it might be possible to spare a day or two from his agricultural endeavours unless some crisis intervened. Even he was not immune to the charm and quality that his Aunt had instantly detected.

Long before Charmian's new wardrobe was complete, the two ladies had settled down to a comfortable working relationship. Charmian had learned that Lady Cecilia's occasional scolds were not meant to be taken too seriously, and that she was completely to be relied upon for guidance in any social dilemma. Lady Cecilia handsomely admitted that her charge had two invaluable assets—a good constitution and an even temper. The one enabled her to endure the long hours of shopping and of standing to be fitted without complaint; the other to refrain from sulks and pettishness when her judgement was over-ruled by the more experienced lady.

"And a pretty wretch I should be to show temper when you have been so good to me," retorted Charmian, obediently relinquishing the opulent green velvet gown that her mentor had rejected as being too old for her. "And you must be for more exhausted than I, since all the responsibility falls on you. Besides, I will confess that I am—am *intoxicated* with London's shops. I don't think that I could ever tire of feasting my eyes on so much beauty."

Pleased by this sincere appreciation, Lady Cecilia nodded stately agreement. But since too much praise is bad for the young she only said rather tartly, "Very likely. But pray do not feast them quite so openly on the various notabilities that

I point out to you. It is desirable that you should be able to recognise people whom you will be for ever meeting at the various functions that you will attend, but to be gazing so raptly at a gentleman just because I chanced to mention that he had been concerned in the defence of Hougoumont is carrying hero worship too far. Why! He might have been the Duke himself! Pray remember that what may be perfectly proper in a schoolgirl is not permissible to a débutante."

Charmian tried to look suitably chastened but could not wholly restrain a giggle. "It's the thought that I am a débutante," she explained apologetically. "I feel more like the old woman on the king's highway—in the nursery rhyme, you know. 'Lawks a'mussy on me, this can not be I.' "

Lady Cecilia wasted no time on such childish frivolity, though she accorded it a tolerant smile. "But it *is* you," she reminded firmly. "And now that you are adequately equipped, it is time to plan our campaign."

Charmian hastily composed her features into an expression of appropriate solemnity. "Yes, ma'am," she said dutifully.

"I have decided that I shall not apply for vouchers for Almack's," announced her duenna briskly. "I daresay they would be granted—since it is I who ask, but it would make for awkwardness. I will not insult your intelligence by pretending that you would find the Assemblies a dead bore. You would, of course, eventually. But not in your first season. The truth of the matter is that a great many questions would be asked to which we do not know the answers."

She noted with approval how Charmian drew herself up at this, the expression of meek docility changing to one of flaring pride, and hurried on before the girl could speak.

"I would be no party to deliberate deception. But to announce the whole truth is to make you an oddity; an object for sympathy, perhaps, but also for speculation and curiosity. Most uncomfortable."

Charmian was reluctantly obliged to acknowledge the truth of this, but the downcast eyes betrayed her feelings.

Lady Cecilia's heart was a good deal softer than her managing ways indicated.

"Come, now. No need for *that* Friday face. It is no great matter, and we shall speak nothing but the truth. The story is that my sister took you in charge after your mother's death, but since she could not leave a sick husband she left the arrangements for your début to me. You have inherited a modest competence but are in no sense an heiress—a fortunate circumstance in one sense, since it would have made our story more complicated."

Charmian could not wholly like it. Too much was being left unsaid. But at least she was not seeking to impose on anyone and she could see that, possibly, to tell the whole story might make things awkward for her kind hostess. She agreed, rather wearily, to Lady Cecilia's version of her history.

And now the invitations began to arrive, along with the answers to those for her own ball, still a fortnight away. Despite Lady Cecilia's careful explanations, half the names were unknown to Charmian. The morning room became a schoolroom to which the two of them repaired after breakfast each day and, with pencil and paper and a copy of Mr. Debrett's Peerage and Baronetage, not to mention some mildly scandalous footnotes supplied by Lady Cecilia, traced out the pedigrees, collaterals and marriage connections of those who had offered or accepted hospitality.

Charmian found it fascinating. Knowing something of the heritage that lay behind the faces added considerably to her interest in her new acquaintances. Possibly her ignorance of her own antecedents increased her enjoyment of other people's, and certainly heredity produced some hilarious surprises. Her own quest had made no progress. Though several people had commented on the quaint pretty name that she bore, no one had been reminded of another Charmian. Nor had any of the older people exclaimed at a resemblance to some friend of bygone days. And, to be truthful, she did not give much thought to the possibility. Life was too full and too absorbing. To be sure she no longer greeted each new acquaintance, each unaccustomed experience, with the uncritical delight that had marked the early days of her love affair with London. The great city itself would always draw her. In a rare moment of fantasy she had thought that it was England's heart; had imagined that, at times, she had felt its thunderous beating. But the rosy, glamorous mist through which at first she had viewed its inhabitants was already dissolving. She had met a number of people to whom she was pleasantly attracted, but there were others who were insipid, shallow or selfish, some who were just plain bores and one or two who were patently untruthful.

So it was with a more discriminating eye that she scanned the pile of invitations that Lady Cecilia had handed over for her perusal while she herself was temporarily engrossed in a letter from her sister. She looked up, smiling, as her hostess folded the sheets together and announced that they seemed to be going on quite prosperously at Medhurst, and held up one of the cards.

"Here's one out of the common run, at least," she announced, her glance returning to the card in her hand. "We are invited, 'To spend an evening in listening to poetry, with, perhaps, a little music.' "

To Charmian's ignorance it was so unusual as to be amusing, set among the abundance of balls, breakfasts and evening receptions (with dancing) like an impudent sparrow in a parade of peacocks. On Lady Cecilia it operated very differently. She said, half incredulous, "Miss Hoborough?"

Charmian glaced again at the card. "Yes. Cheyne Walk."

"Chainy Walk," corrected Lady Cecilia automatically, her face positively ecstatic. "My dear, this is beyond anything great. I must confess that I had hoped—which is why I invited Stanton Hoborough to your ball. Her nephew, you know. But one can never rely upon her behaving exactly like other people, and although our families were pretty well acquainted she is a good deal older than I."

Charmian could see little cause for this excessive gratification. The entertainment offered struck her as decidedly fusty. But this, she was promptly informed, was a grave social error. An invitation to Miss Hoborough's Chelsea home was more highly to be prized than one to Carlton House.

"Her salon is *most* exclusive," explained Lady Cecilia, "which is really rather amusing when one recalls the revolutionary sentiments for which she was notorious in her salad days."

"Truly?" queried Charmian, much intrigued.

"Yes indeed. Though in all fairness one is bound to acknowledge that at that time it was all the crack to be a revolutionary, in a mild, idealistic sort of way. Even our present Poet Laureate was influenced by republican beliefs, and many of our writers and politicians likewise. They discarded them pretty quickly when they discovered what revolution meant in practical terms. Mr. Southey, for one, is a stout Tory nowadays, and I daresay that Miss Hoborough, too, has had a similar change of heart. Inheritance of vast wealth is apt to change one's point of view. But that is old history. Your inclusion in her invitation could not have been more providential. No need to fret over vouchers for Almack's if Miss Hoborough takes you up. I confess that I find the intellectual atmosphere a little above me, but it gives one a tremendous cachet to be seen at her parties. And the entertainment will be of the highest professional kind. No fumbling amateurs for Miss Hoborough. You will hear a Siddons or a Viotti. The most famous virtuosi fall over themselves to oblige her. I really don't know how she does it. Of course she is a great patron of the arts, as well as being related to everyone who *is* anyone, but still" —her voice trailed off as she pondered the mystery of Miss Hoborough's influential position.

SIX

IT WAS IRONIC, THOUGHT ROLF HERIOT
grimly, that after such a disastrous spring the
weather should choose to smile on the occasion of
his aunt's ball. To be sure it made his journey to
Town so much the easier—but if only they could
have had a little of this fickle sunshine earlier in the
year! The lambing flock had suffered badly in the
severe wintry conditions, with snow and hail per-
sisting through April; and the prospect for the hay
harvest was bleak. Where the meadows were not
water-logged, the grass had been laid flat. It was
small comfort that the whole country was suffering
under the same affliction; that every one was agreed
that this first summer of the peace had produced
the worst weather of the century. He himself was
better placed than his neighbours since at least he
had no wheat to worry about. What would become
of *that* he did not care to speculate. Certainly for
Ryelands there would be no profits this season.

Lucky if he could pull through without running into debt. If he had not had several business matters awaiting his attention in Town he thought he would probably have begged off. He had an amused, mildly protective liking for Charmian Tracy but she would doubtless manage well enough without him and he was not in the mood for light-hearted revelry.

It was a sober-faced gentleman who surrendered the reins to a waiting groom and presently greeted his Aunt Cecilia with due civility. She welcomed him kindly if rather distractedly, expressing her gratitude for his support on this important occasion in the intervals of directing a baize-aproned underling as to the proper placing of some potted palms and assuring an agitated housekeeper that certainly the pastries from Gunter's had been ordered. No doubt they were just a little delayed. He agreed that it was *most* fortunate that the weather had decided to favour the event, accepted one or two playful jibes at his bucolic fanaticism with good humour and declined an offer of refreshment.

"Which is just as well," declared his aunt candidly, "for dear alone knows what they would have sent up for you. Anyone would imagine that we were not in the way of giving large parties, which I can assure you is *not* the case, though I suppose it is three or four years since we gave a set ball. I have put you in Jasper's room by the way. I had hoped that he might have been here—one can never have too many gentlemen at a ball—but he writes that his furlough is delayed. Charmian is probably still in the Chinese drawing room. I asked her to make sure that all was in order there. For the card players, you know. Though why any one should come to a ball and expect to play cards I can never understand. But so it is, and your uncle vows he won't have them in the library." And she bustled away happily with a reminder that luncheon would be served in an hour's time. "Though I fear it will be remarkable chiefly for its frugality," she sighed.

He had no engagements until after luncheon. It might be amusing to discover what Miss Tracy made of London. He strolled into the Chinese drawing room, viewing its ornate furnishing with mild distaste. Aunt Cecilia might deride his homespun preferences and insist that it was all the crack, but give him the mellow antiquity of Medhurst, even the stark simplicity of Ryelands, rather than this exotic stuff, though he was obliged to concede that the atmosphere was cheerful and welcoming. Perhaps the half dozen card tables that were disposed about it had succeeded in depressing its pretensions to oriental splendour.

One table, however, was not set out for cards. It supported an elegant arrangement of irises, yellow and purple-brown, so placed that it was reflected in the mirrors that hung over the twin hearths, and kneeling beside this creation of the florist's art was a young lady whom, at first glance, Mr. Heriot would not have recognised.

Intent on her task she had not noticed his approach, and for a few moments he was able to study her changed appearance and wonder how it had been achieved. Her hair looked different, he thought vaguely, thus cursorily dismissing the artistry with which the unruly curls had been disciplined, skilfully cut and styled to show the shape of the head and accentuate its proud poise. She had always been neatly and appropriately dressed—save on one memorable occasion—and to his uninstructed eye her morning gown was not excessively smart, though its amber-gold hue certainly presented a charming picture as she knelt beside the irises. How was a mere man to know that Madame Fayette herself had supervised the cutting and fitting of that 'plain' gown, approved the choice of the glowing colour?

Was there an air of self-sufficiency? A new reserve? Certainly he could trace little of the naive, confiding child in today's coolly poised society maiden. London had already left its mark. A footman came in with some message, and she dealt with it almost casually. He could not hear the actual exchange but her abstracted expression and the careless tilt of her head were sufficient indication that London servants no longer held any terrors for her.

That was as it should be. Yet he was dimly aware of a sense of disappointment, almost of loss, as he crossed the room towards her, speaking her name quietly so that he should not startle her. At the sound of his voice she scrambled to her feet, turning eagerly towards him in welcome, the outstretched hands, the face of delight recalling immediately the girl he had learned to like so well. No trace of the well-drilled débutante in *that* greeting.

She said joyously, "You are come earlier than I expected. How splendid! Now there will be time to hear all the news before we are caught up in to-night's festivities. Come and walk in the garden with me. It is a shame to be indoors when the sun is shining at last."

His mood lifted to match hers. "Your news—or mine?" he queried. "I doubt yours will make more cheerful hearing. The country bumpkin has little to rehearse but a catalogue of woes. Hail—snow—unseasonable frost—wind and rain, we have had them all. But how have matters gone with you?"

She scarcely heard the enquiry, her expression grave, concerned. "I have thought of you often," she said simply. "One of my school friends lives in the Scottish border country since she married. She wrote that they had lost most of their lambs in a great storm and I wondered then how you were faring, though of course Mary's home is much further north. Has it been very bad?"

"Bad enough." He shrugged. "And I have come off lightly compared to some of my neighbours. Still, if the weather mends now"—he glanced up at the soft blue of the sky—"we may yet salvage something of the hay crop. But come! This is my holiday—and you are failing sadly in your social obligations. You should be entertaining me with all the latest talk of the Town or even indulging me with a little playful flirtation rather than encouraging me to bore you with my troubles. Am I to have the privilege of standing up with you tonight? I am sadly out of practice but I think I can be trusted to keep my place in the set and to remember the sequence of the figures."

She would have preferred to hear more of his difficulties at Ryelands, but since he obviously wished to change the subject it would have been discourteous to persist. She told him, instead, of some of her earlier experiences under his aunt's roof. And since she had the knack of sketching a personality in a few words, a Puckish sense of humour and a lively enjoyment of the joke that turned against herself, it was not long before she had the satisfaction of seeing his sombre mood yield to frank amusement. It was on a note of comfortable accord that they went in to lunch, but there was no further opportunity for private conversation. As soon as the meal was over Mr. Heriot went off about his own affairs while a reluctant Charmian went meekly to her room to rest upon her bed in preparation for the evening's exertions.

Rolf was surprised by the pleasurable anticipation with which he dressed for his aunt's party. This was a new come-out for him, he reflected amusedly, studying his tall figure in his cousin's pier glass. His evening rig was pretty well, he decided. Not of the latest cut, of course, but still retaining something of its pristine distinction since he so rarely had occasion to wear it. Though what he was doing studying his reflection in a mirror like some simpering girl he could not imagine, except, naturally, that one would not wish to put Aunt Cecilia to the blush.

She was a good soul, Aunt Cecilia. Had her foibles—as who had not? But sound as a roast at heart. Not many matrons of her standing would have behaved so generously to a nameless waif. Sincerely he hoped that tonight's expectations would be amply fulfilled; that she would have the success that she so confidently anticipated.

He need not have been anxious. A little conscience stricken because of the reticence that she had felt obliged to observe over Charmian's story, her ladyship had unwittingly overdone her insistence on the girl's lack of fortune. There was certainly nothing purse-pinched in her appearance, and it was known that she had been expensively educated. In these circumstance Lady Cecilia's repeated protestations had produced a result the exact opposite of the one she had intended. Presently one or two wiseacres had put their heads together. Doing it rather too brown, they decided. Daresay her ladyship only wanted to protect the girl against fortune hunters, but it was not to be expected that *they* should swallow such an improbable tale. If marriage contracts were in question, then obviously one would enquire more precisely into Miss Tracy's circumstances. Meanwhile, let her careful guardian preserve her little fabrication if it soothed her. The girl had excellent style. She did not put herself forward at all and actually seemed to *enjoy* listening to her elders talking of days gone by. If she was not precisely beautiful she was still an appealing little creature with an air of innocence all too rare these days and a wistful charm that touched even a cynical heart. Society was prepared to take her to its fickle bosom, and the gentle ripple of amusement caused by Lady Cecilia's dissimulation worked strongly in her favour.

In fact, for once in her life, she might well have scored a success on appearance alone. Lady Cecilia and Madame Fayette had conferred long and earnestly over her gown. They had eventually decided that since she was rather older than the usual débutante a touch of colour might be permissible rather than the traditional white, and after much deliberation had selected a heavy China silk in a delicate shade of green. Fortunately Charmian had been so bemused by the beauty of the supple, carelessly heaped folds that she had forgotten to question the price. Fortunately, too, her mentors were at once agreed that so beautiful a material needed no adornment. The plainest possible style would be best for so small and slight a girl. Tiny puff sleeves and a high waist, so that the long line of the skirt would make her look taller, and just a single ruffle of the silk to edge the low decolletage. The finished effect had caused Lady Cecilia to sigh contentedly. "You have a very good skin, my dear," she approved, "and against the green——"

Madame Fayette was even more convincing. She actually forgot her pseudo-French phrases and genteel accent. In purest Houndsditch she said fervently, "Cor, ducks! Yer looks a proper treat. Yer do strite!" And was quite unconscious of her lapse.

Tonight, surveying the completed toilet, from the silver cords threaded in Grecian style through the artlessly piled curls to the little green slippers, noting the pretty colour that excitement had brought to the soft cheeks and the glow in the big dark eyes, Lady Cecilia expressed her satisfaction in more felicitous phrases.

"You look quite charmingly. I hope that you will enjoy an evening of unalloyed pleasure. Remains only to give you my small token to mark the occasion. No," as Charmian would have protested, "it is the merest trifle, but it matches your dress. I can scarcely remember the uncle who gave it to me. I was still in leading strings and have rarely worn it. Green is not my colour."

It was a pendant of jade, carved to simulate a single rhododendron blossom. Lady Cecilia fastened the delicate silver chain about the girl's throat. The shaggy petals glowed startlingly green against the white skin. With her usual discrimination, Lady

Cecilia had added the perfect finishing touch. Unpretentious but unusual, the pendant drew the eye irresistibly.

Mr. Heriot received Charmian's appearance with a mixture of astonishment and proprietory pride. Who would have thought the child could look so lovely? Small wonder that she was besieged by eager suppliants for every dance. She danced well, too, he noticed. He went off to do his duty by less fortunate damsels.

He found it surprisingly tedious, though he was obliged to acknowledge that the fault lay with himself. He had not seen any of the current theatrical attractions nor attended any of the fashionable 'squeezes'—was, in fact, hopelessly out of touch with the London scene—and so was sadly handicapped in point of conversation on the accepted ballroom topics. He was able to agree that the resemblance between the Appleton twins was quite remarkable, and to listen politely to several anecdotes based on this circumstance, but after the third repetition even this subject palled. There was some relief to be found in exchanging greetings with one or two of the chaperones who wished to enquire how his father did and to send affectionate messages to his mother. He wished that he had thought to ask Charmian for more than one dance, or at least of suggesting that she should go down to supper with him. As it was he was obliged to see her pass on Stanton Hoborough's arm, not even remarking his presence, absorbed in some bantering exchange with her escort.

But his one dance with her was worth waiting for, he decided contentedly. It was a waltz, and despite the disparity in height they found that their steps suited well. And there was opportunity for such private talk as quadrilles and country dances made impossible. Charmian's pleasure, too, was infectious. It had been a wonderful evening. Every one had been so kind. He would think her odiously conceited if she told him even half the flattering things that had been said about her dress and her dancing.

"Then I shall not bore you with further repetition," he retorted, slipping easily into their old informality. "But tell me, what fortune with your quest?"

She shook her head. "None. I have almost ceased to think of it." And then, a little shyly. "Perhaps I had come to refine too much on my situation, being much alone with few distractions. Now there are so many people—so much to do. And sometimes, too, I remember what your mother said, and know that I would rather be nameless than be obliged to acknowledge kinship with some of the people I meet."

They circled the room again, her short-lived solemnity swiftly dispelled by the lilting music. There was mischief in her face as she said, "And think of the advantages! If I were a young lady of impeccable pedigree I should not be permitted to enjoy this waltz. Not unless some haughty dame at Almack's had signified her approval."

He smiled. "And you *are* enjoying it?"

"Very much. Though I am very sorry that we have not had more opportunity of talking. There are so many things I want to know. Whether you have been to Medhurst recently and how they go on there. If you have thought any more about breeding horses. You mentioned it once, I remember. Some special kind, developed by a man called Bakewell."

He could not help smiling as he compared her eager interest with the stilted conversations in which he had played so inept a part earlier in the evening. But the music was quickening to its climax and there was no time for further exchanges. He found himself quite reluctant to surrender his partner. On a sudden impulse he said, "If you are not too tired, perhaps you would drive with me in the Park tomorrow morning. I cannot, in any case, leave before noon—papers to be signed which cannot be ready earlier. That would give us ample opportunity to talk. Without continual interruption," he concluded in some exasperation as her next partner came up to claim her.

SEVEN

ALTHOUGH IT HAD BEEN PAST THREE o'clock when she put her candle out, Charmian woke at her usual time, and with that instant awareness of something pleasant impending that had always marked a birthday or some long-promised treat. She lay relaxed for a few moments, reluctant to wake properly yet seeking drowsily to remember what had prompted this sense of joyous anticipation, and presently the sound of wheels rattling along the street gave her the clue. Of course! She was to drive in the Park with Mr. Heriot.

Fully awake now, she contemplated the merits of her several carriage dresses. Because of the inclement weather there had been few opportunities of wearing these. The green cambric was the prettiest —but she had worn green last night. Perhaps the brown, with the little fur-edged cape.

But these happy deliberations were brought to an abrupt end when Katy tapped gently on her door to enquire if she would like to take breakfast in bed. "Milady thought you'd be glad of the rest, miss, after last night. She's staying in bed herself, and she says you've no engagements until this evening. It's too wet to go out, any way."

The last dregs of drowsiness were effectively dispelled. Charmian sat up and exclaimed, "Wet? Oh no!"

But Katy had already drawn back the curtains to expose windows streaming with rain that showed no intention of accommodating itself to Miss Tracy's wishes. The prospect of breakfasting lazily but alone was unattractive. With a memory of the early hours that Mr. Heriot had kept at Medhurst, she announced that she would dress at once and breakfast downstairs. The amber-gold dress that she had worn yesterday was her favourite morning dress and would add a note of colour to this grey morning. Katy, a friendly little creature, told her that it brought out the lighter tones in her hair and added, for good measure, that it was a real treat to dress natural curls and not to have to heat the tongs or fret as to whether the curl would hold.

These homely compliments were very acceptable for despite the ease with which she had slipped into place in the fashionable world, Charmian was still diffident about her own looks. Mama's plaintive comments about her deficiencies in this respect had left an indelible impression. So the simple praise was sweet in her ears and it was in more cheerful mood that she ran lightly downstairs and pushed open the door of the breakfast parlour.

Mr. Heriot was before her. He seemed to have finished his breakfast and was standing in the window gloomily watching the steadily falling rain as he drank his coffee, but as he turned to greet her his expression lightened and there was amused appreciation in his voice as he said, "No one to look at you would imagine that you did not seek your bed till long after midnight. I did not expect to see you for another couple of hours. I'm afraid this rain means business and there will be no chance of that drive in the Park."

He pulled out her chair and attended to her needs, carving delicately thin slices from a fine York ham when she said that she was quite shockingly hungry.

"I didn't eat very much supper," she confessed. "I expect I was too excited."

He smiled. "Small wonder. Mama will be delighted to hear of your triumph. No less a person than Stanton Hoborough to take you in to supper. Aunt Cecilia has been pulling strings to some purpose, but not even *she* can have anticipated that he would single you out for such distinguished attention."

"Oh dear!" said Charmian is some dismay. "I had not realised that he was of any particular importance. To speak truth I did not like him above half. I wasn't actually discourteous but I certainly didn't exert myself to please. Is it *very* bad?"

He looked amused. "Of course not. I daresay it would do him a great deal of good. He has not come very much in my way but I believe he is a general favourite with the ladies and regarded as a very eligible parti, since he stands to inherit his aunt's fortune."

Charmian mulled this over. "I expect I was the one at fault," she acknowledged. "He was perfectly affable and very amusing. But although he made me laugh, I thought his remarks about the company were malicious—even downright unkind."

"A good many people do that," he said sympathetically, "and win an undeserved reputation for wit by making game of their fellows."

"I couldn't help wondering what he would say about *me* to his next partner," she admitted.

They discussed the ball at some length but drifted eventually to other topics. Mr. Heriot had paid one brief visit to Medhurst since Charmian had left and was able to answer her eager questions about the household, a little surprised that she had come to know them so well on such short acquaintance and obviously held them in some affection. For her part, Charmian could not help contrasting his laughing account of one of those Homeric encounters between Nan and Susan with Mr. Hoborough's style. But then—Mr. Hoborough would never have concerned himself with such humble folk.

"Mama says it would be most unkind to part the pair of them," he concluded, "and as, naturally, she could not dream of depriving you of Susan's services, the only solution that she can suggest is that you should make your home at Medhurst. When you are weary of the delights of Town, of course."

Charmian smiled, though there was a small aching lump in her throat and it was a husky voice that said slowly, "If your Mama owned Blenheim I doubt if it would house all the forlorn creatures that she would like to shelter and comfort. It is as well that she has you to check some of her impulsive starts—though at times it must be an unpleasant duty. Besides giving strangers an unfortunate impression of your personality," she ended on a note of demure mischief.

Mr. Heriot was denied the opportunity of taking her up on this head, one of the maids coming in with a message from Mrs. Everett—Lady Cecilia's formidable housekeeper. Would Miss Tracy mind sitting in the library, just for this morning? They were putting the salons to rights as quickly as possible but there was still a good deal to be done. And since it was such a miserable day, she had caused the library fire to be lit.

Not even Mrs. Everett, of course, presumed to suggest that Mr. Heriot, also, should betake himself to the library out of the way of the workers, but that gentleman obligingly exclaimed, "And an excellent notion, too. May I join you there, Miss Tracy? A game of chess, perhaps, or a hand of piquet, instead of our drive."

But Charmian, who was totally ignorant of chess and a tyro at card games, preferred rather to show him some books on farming that she had discovered. He followed her obediently, touched and amused by this childishly palpable attempt to provide him with suitable entertainment.

The books were tucked away like some guilty secret on the top shelf in the darkest corner of the library and proved to be a very mixed collection. They ranged from a rare copy of Tusser's 'Hundreth Good Pointes of Husbandrie', published in 1557, to some very up-to-date accounts of the proceedings of the Bath and West of England Agricultural Society. Charmian, explaining that she knew exactly where to put her hand on them, mounted the library steps and handed down book after book to be spread out on the table. Then both stooped to survey the motley collection.

"Nothing of Coke's," said Rolf with regret.

Charmian looked up enquiringly.

"Thomas Coke, of Holkham Hall in Norfolk," he elaborated. "A great agriculturist. But above all, a practical man—so perhaps he hasn't published his theories. He is of Bracewell's school of thought, though, and I would dearly have loved to meet him, even through the medium of the printed page, having heard so much of the improvements he has made at Holkham. It is not so far away, either. Conditions must be similar to mine at Ryelands. I wonder how he is faring this year?"

They browsed companionably through the books, smiling over Tusser's doggerel verses with their comical mixture of country lore and worldly wisdom. Rolf shook his head. "And at that, poor fellow, he was a better poet than he was a farmer."

Charmian was surprised. "You knew of him, then?"

"But of course! He, too, farmed in Suffolk. At Cattiwade. But he was not overly successful. And Bakewell, for all his knowledge and skill and the large sums of money that he made, was bankrupt before he died. No man can rely on making his fortune from the land, be he never so diligent, though Coke seems to have made a success of Holkham. They say his rent-roll has increased tenfold since he inherited, and that just by plain good management."

"But I daresay it cost a deal of money to do it," suggested Charmian thoughtfully. "Susan says that money breeds money. I'm sure you could do just as well if you were not hampered by considerations of expense."

Her understanding and her interest were forever surprising him, little slip of a thing that she was. And he found her faith in his abilities quite ridiculously comforting. He would have like to fling a careless arm round those slender shoulders and hug her affectionately for her loyalty to one who had really no claim to it. But of course she was *not* his sister, and such a demonstration would be quite improper.

Charmian had begun to arrange the books in their proper order prior to replacing them, but her hands moved slowly, her mind only partly on her task.

"All the same, you are really very fortunate," she said suddenly.

"That you must certainly prove to me," he returned. "It will take a deal of doing, but should make interesting hearing."

She eyed him straitly, for she was wholly serious and inclined to resent the suggestion of mockery. Her voice was cool as she said, "You were born to high rank and have been trained from childhood in the discipline of responsibility. You know just what needs to be done and how best it may be achieved. But instead of falling heir to a flourishing estate, where I daresay you would have been moped to death half the time with nothing to do, you are faced with the task of building up a new prosperity. Half the gentlemen I meet are concerned with nothing more vital than the cut of a coat, the choice of a waistcoat and the pursuit of their various sporting amusements. It seems to me a very boring, not to say useless existence."

She hesitated briefly as though sorting out her ideas, and when she went on again the infectious warmth was back in face and voice. "When I was small, Susan used to tell me stories of the early settlers in Virginia; of the difficulties and the hardships that they had to contend with. I think your life is a little like theirs. To be sure you don't have the interest and excitement of exploring a strange new country—but neither do you have to face hostile Indians. You have a much loved home and family and an acknowledged place in the world, and the task you have set yourself is infinitely worth while. It seems to me that in many ways you are to be envied."

She looked very sweet and lovable in her earnestness, the big brown eyes appealing for his understanding. Rolf was aware of a strong impulse to take her in his arms and conclude the argument with kisses and realised in one swift flash that his desire was in no sense brotherly and that somehow it must be restrained. Hastily, with the best assumption of lightness that he could muster, he said, "At least we are in agreement on one head. I should certainly dislike such a life of idleness as you describe. But you must have been singularly unfortunate in your masculine acquaintance. Are there no politicians, no military men among your court? They, surely, might command your respect."

So abrupt and clumsy a change of subject could only be construed as a deliberate snub. Charmian realised that her homily—for as such it now appeared to her—must have sounded intolerably presumptuous. Small wonder it had brought on her so crushing a set-down. Her cheeks burned and she had to press her lips tightly together to stop the betraying quiver of her chin. Hastily she picked up the nearest books and turned towards the steps so that he should not see her face. She declined his suggestion that he was better able for the toilsome task, saying that she was more familiar with the order in which they should be placed, profoundly thankful that her voice was steady enough to hide her distress.

Rolf handed up the heavier volumes mechanically, shaken quite off balance by the discovery that all unawares he had tumbled headlong into love. Deep in his consciousness was the knowledge that, whatever his emotions, he was in no position to marry, but at the moment he was more concerned with recalling the more memorable incidents of his brief acquaintance with Charmian. Charmian in his mother's antiquated gown, her eyes daring him to laugh at her; Charmian brushing out Mama's still abundant hair, the pair of them chuckling over some obscure feminine joke. Charmian waltzing in his arms, the faint sweet scent of her skin teasing his nostrils.

He gave her the last book and watched as she painstakingly aligned and spaced the collection. How could he guess that her eyes were misty with unshed tears? That she was deliberately postponing the moment when she must descend from her lofty sanctuary and face him?

Perhaps it was this agony of self-consciousness

that caused her to miss the last step so that she landed awkwardly and might have fallen if Rolf had not been at hand to steady her. Poor Rolf! In general he was reasonably adept at presenting an unmoved front in the face of fortune's whims, but coming hard on the heels of his startling discovery, this was the last straw. She was here, in his arms, his small sweet love. Propriety and his circumstances alike forgotten, he made no attempt to help her to a conveniently placed chair. Instead he gathered her closer and exclaimed anxiously, foolishly, "You're not hurt, beloved?"

She was not hurt at all, but the shock of that last word took her breath away, so that she could only stare at him in a mixture of disbelief and dawning delight. He was *not* angry with her. Instead the concern and tenderness in his voice seemed to turn her whole world upside down. It gave her a blissful feeling of belonging. She looked up at him shyly, her mouth curved to a wondering, vulnerable little half smile.

Without a second thought, Rolf stooped and kissed her. And since she made no protest but rather nestled closer in his hold, the kiss lasted some time. After which it seemed the most natural thing in the world to smooth gentle lips over her eyelids and temples. There was a hint of a dimple in one cheek that must be duly saluted and then once again that soft beguiling mouth.

Only this time it was different. Charmian might

be wholly untaught, but she was young and ardent and hungry for affection. Moreover she had recovered from her first surprise. She gave a little sigh of content, and returned his kiss with what could only be described as enthusiasm, while one small hand came up behind his head as though to hold him to her.

It was her innocent response that gave him pause. It brought home to him the full iniquity of his conduct. Taking advantage of a child who had some sort of claim on his protection was bad enough. If he permitted her to betray some small partiality for him, it would be unforgiveable. Reluctantly, but firmly, he put her from him, still supporting her with one arm while he drew forward a chair for her.

"You did not twist your ankle?" he said curtly. And when she shook her head went on at once, "I hope that you will try to bring yourself to forgive me, little as I deserve it. My father would say I should be horse-whipped for insulting you so. I can only plead irresistible temptation—you are so very sweet and so lovely—and promise that I will not err again."

Silence, while he stood submissively before her awaiting judgement, his mouth compressed to a hard line, his hands tightly clenched at his sides. It was difficult to believe that this stern-faced man had held her in his arms and kissed her so tenderly. She supposed that he *had* behaved badly—but so had she. A well-bred maiden would undoubtedly have screamed or swooned at that first kiss. Miss Tracy had felt no such inclination. In fact the less said about her inclinations the better, she decided ruefully. She would consider *them* later. Meanwhile he was waiting, and she must say *something*. Well— she would neither dissemble nor stoop to a conventional scolding.

"It would be difficult to be angry with any gentleman who had just told me I was irresistibly lovely," she pointed out. "In any case I see nothing so dreadful in your behaviour." Her chin came up and she blushed rosily, but she brought the words out bravely enough. "In fact I l-liked it!"

Rolf's rigid attitude relaxed. Bless the child! She really was a darling, even though that honesty of hers must oblige him to say things that he would have preferred to leave unsaid.

"You do me too much honour," he said quietly, and bowed formally over her hand, brushing the slim fingers with his lips. "And you are much too generous," he added more simply, smiling down at her. "But that is like you. It is a fortunate circumstance that I must go back to Ryelands tonight so that you will be spared the embarrassment of my continued presence. There is a party tonight, too, isn't there? A ridotto, at the Melling's. I trust it will serve to distract your thoughts from my presumptuous behaviour." That would surely underline the fact that the brief madness was over and that no more need be said.

It did not serve for Charmian. "And in future you will avoid me as much as possible and set me at a distance if we *should* chance to meet?" she said soberly.

"Better so, my darling." The endearment slipped out despite him. "If I thought that your happiness lay in my keeping—but you know as well as I do that I cannot afford to marry while I have Medhurst on my hands. With all the distractions that surround you, you will soon forget me."

There could be two opinions about *that*, thought Charmian, but pride forbade further protest. And in truth she was not sure of her own feelings. The whole thing had come upon her too quickly. She was still bewildered by the sensations that had sprung to life within her at Rolf's kiss, and much inclined to distrust them. She said quietly, "Very well. We shall be obliged to meet again at luncheon, but I trust that we shall be able to do so with reasonable composure." On which dignified note she favoured him with a slight curtsey and walked sedately out of the room.

EIGHT

THERE WAS LITTLE TIME FOR BROODING over the surprising things that could happen in a respectable library on a wet morning. Since the weather continued unkind, several picnic parties had to be cancelled and one alfresco breakfast which *was* blessed by fitful sunshine ended in a storm which drenched most of the guests. But the succession of rout parties, musical soirées, dress balls, plays and concerts more than made up for this lack. Charmian heard people bewailing the impossibility of arranging any form of outdoor entertainment and wondered how they would have found the time for it if the weather *had* been favourable. As it was she was obliged to change her dress three and four times in a day and was never in bed before midnight.

Having decided that in general her protegée's taste in dress was to be relied upon, Lady Cecilia rarely interfered with her choice, but on the day of

Miss Hoborough's reception she began fussing at breakfast time.

"I would like you to wear the peach-blossom satin tonight, my dear," she said seriously. "And I will lend you my coral set to go with it. Just the necklace and a bracelet, you know. Very simple and girlish, but the colour will bring out the richer tones of the satin and the whole ensemble will serve to remind your hostess of her own girlhood without being impossibly outdated. If she can see you at all, poor thing. She is very near blind, alas! Some kind of a film over the eyes—a cataract I think they call it. Which reminds me—do not be alarmed or distressed if she seems to peer very closely into your face. She is apt to do so with new acquaintances. But there! I daresay she will not single you out for any particular notice, and perhaps that would be as well. She is very outspoken and can, at times, be downright embarrassing."

Her ladyship should have given more thought to this characteristic. She might then have deferred their arrival in Cheyne Walk until Miss Hoborough's rooms were so crammed with company that newcomers were inconspicuous. As it was they were early—and their hostess was able to bestow her whole attention upon them.

She was not much taller than Charmian, and so thin that she looked almost emaciated, but she wore her plum-coloured satin and her diamonds right regally. The white hair piled high on her head in the fashion of her youth added to her stature and an aristocratic beak of a nose and a determined jaw suggested that it might be wiser to repress the stirring of compassion evoked by that strained, searching gaze. Miss Hoborough might not be able to see very clearly in the physical sense but mentally she was very wide awake.

Her greeting to Lady Cecilia was brusquely friendly and she turned at once to Charmian, extending a slender white hand on which two magnificent rings hung loose and heavy. Charmian curtsied. Miss Hoborough's cool firm fingers drew her closer. She peered into the girl's face, shook her head and sighed a little and said, in a voice that could have wooed the birds from the trees, "Forgive an old woman's curiosity, child. I cannot see you clearly—as doubtless your careful chaperone has already warned you—though *this* pretty trinket I both see and recognise."

Her free hand came up to touch the coral bracelet that Charmian wore. "*You* wore that, Cecil—it must be thirty years ago! How such trifles take one back! But since I cannot see you, Miss Tracy, will you not tell me a little about yourself? What my nephew has told me about you arouses my liveliest curiosity. 'Not strictly pretty in the fashionable way,' says he, 'but attractive and unusual.' It is rare indeed to hear him praise anyone so high. I could only surmise that you had not fallen worshipping at his feet, as so many of the foolish chits do. I suppose it is too much to hope that you actually snubbed him?"

Before the embarrassed Charmian could frame a reply, she was off again. "Related to the Medhursts, I collect. Which *does* surprise me, for I have known Philip Heriot since he was a scrubby schoolboy and have never heard of any relations called Tracy. But perhaps the connection is through your mother. What was her maiden name?"

This naturally cast both her guests into confusion, and though she could not see the dismay in their faces she was quick to sense the slight, awkward pause, and to catch the swift turn of Charmian's head as the girl sought her chaperone's guidance. Some mystery here, she reflected happily. People, with their foibles and their secrets, were still her abiding delight, and though the tenets of hospitality forbade her to embarrass her guests further, she promised herself the satisfaction of enquiring into Miss Tracy's family history at a more convenient time. Meanwhile she was almost as relieved as the two conspirators when the arrival of more guests obliged her to break off the conversation. The Castlereaghs added distinction even to *her* party. To be sure the great statesman's popularity was sadly diminished nowadays—and not a year since Waterloo was won! But what should Miss Hoborough care for the fickle favour of the mindless masses? She accounted his lordship both enlightened and farsighted and she, at any rate, would show that she valued these qualities. With a word of apology to her companions and an alarming promise that later they would enjoy a comfortable talk together, she surged forward to greet the new arrivals.

Despite its intimidating opening, Charmian found herself enjoying the evening. The entertainment, as Lady Cecilia had promised, was superior, the company distinguished. Most of the guests were a good deal older than Charmian so it seemed natural that Mr. Hoborough should devote a good deal of his time to her, pointing out several celebrities among the guests and telling her various anecdotes in which they figured. She found him more likeable in his rôle as host, and there was a subtle flattery in the accuracy with which he remembered her favourite dishes at supper. With a wary eye on her hostess lest she should be trapped into that 'comfortable' talk she watched and listened and occasionally put in a comment of her own, and thought how she would be able to savour the memory of this brilliant company when her own brief social flight was done.

It was not until they went to take leave of their hostess that she was abruptly recalled to reality. Miss Hoborough smiled at her in the kindest way and regretted that they had not had time to improve their acquaintance.

"But I have had an excellent notion about that," she went on. "You shall come to my birthday ball. I daresay you think that is an odd sort of entertainment for such an antiquated female, but I think you will enjoy it. It is a costume ball and all young girls like dressing up. You will be invited to wear the style of dress that was fashionable in my hey-day. Vastly becoming, I promise you. You will be back at Medhurst by then, so it will be quite convenient. Unless you were planning to take her with you to Brighton, Cecil?"

"Oh no!" said Lady Cecilia placidly. "My privilege ends with the Season. Mary is longing to have her back at Medhurst. I can see the pair of us coming to cuffs as to where she is to spend Christmas!" She glanced at Charmian's troubled face. "You are greatly privileged, my love. Miss Hoborough's costume balls are famous. You will like it of all things."

"Mary must tear herself from Philip's side for once, and the two of you shall stay the night so that we can spend a lazy day recovering from our exertions," planned Miss Hoborough cheerfully.

It was not the time or the place for Charmian to explain that her future plans were uncertain. She thanked her hostess very prettily, saying all that was proper about the suggested treat and trusting that Lady Cecilia would be able to suggest a valid excuse.

Lady Cecilia had no such intention. "Nonsense, child! Mary will tell her as much of your story as she thinks necessary, and she will be no more shocked than we were. She has flouted convention all her days and I dare swear she'll offer you neither pity nor patronage. Rather she will find your story intriguing—a puzzle that she would like to solve. You might find her managing ways something of a trial, though, if she *does* decide to take you under her wing. For a Republican she is absurdly imperious."

Miss Hoborough was not alone in that respect, thought Charmian, smiling a little in the darkness of the carriage. Even Lady Medhurst, gentle and affectionate as she was, had meddled in Charmian's affairs in a distinctly high-handed manner. But it was obvious that further argument would be useless at the moment. She lapsed into silence; and, as so often in these brief intervals of reflection, her thoughts returned to that strange experience in the library. If only she could consult Mr. Heriot; not only about such minor difficulties as this invitation, but also about the looming problem of the future. It had been impossible to keep an exact account of all the monies that had been expended on the various requirements of her London Season but she knew that they must amount to a considerable sum. It was time to call a halt. There would have to be a reckoning, and presumably it would have to be with Mr. Sanbury, Mama's lawyer, since she could scarcely seek out a gentleman who was at pains to shun her society. Nor, for the same reason, could she accept the invitation to make her home at Medhurst.

If only she was rich! Mr. Heriot had certainly

implied that his own straitened means and nothing else had prevented him from making her an offer. He must love her very much, she thought shyly, if he was prepared to overlook her doubtful ancestry, while she. . . . In the darkness of the carriage she blushed hotly at the memory of those kisses.

But dreaming impossible dreams and dwelling on remembered bliss was no way to plan a future. Sternly she reminded herself of the facts. It was not until Rolf had spoken of having Medhurst on his hands that she had realised the full extent of his difficulties. But of course. Shorn of its farms, the old house could not possibly be self-supporting. No doubt the profits from Ryelands were regularly diverted to the maintenance of Medhurst. Charmian did not suppose for a moment that Rolf begrudged them. But it must be maddening at times to see money so hardly earned and so sorely needed squandered on a frivolous whim or even expended on a generous impulse. She could not endure the thought that she should add to his burdens.

The Season was coming to an end. They still had several engagements, but some families had already closed their Town houses and betaken themselves to the country or to some fashionable watering place.

"And damned cold they'll find it," pronounced Sir George jovially, glancing out at skies that remained persistently leaden and a flag-way that gleamed with recent rain. "Ruination to the crops, this weather. They were saying at the Club that there's places where the wheat still hasn't sprouted." He proceeded to enquire into his wife's plans for leaving Town, making a note of the date in his pocket book and telling her that he supposed she must have her way but that it would be far more sensible to stay snug at home. "Not," he added slyly, with a quizzical twinkle at Charmian, "that we should be allowed to enjoy it in peace. No sooner did the word reach Brighton and Worthing that Miss Tracy was still in Town than we should have all your beaux posting back again before the cat could lick her ear. Tell me, m'dear. Among so many, can you not find *one* to take your fancy?"

One could not resent such teasing from kind Sir George. He had, in fact, been quite put about by being obliged to explain to certain hopeful gentlemen that he was not Miss Tracy's guardian and could do nothing to further their matrimonial ambitions.

Lady Cecilia intervened. "She is very right in refusing to make up her mind too quickly. Marriage is a solemn undertaking. And a girl is entitled to enjoy her first season. I would not wish you to earn a reputation for *flirting*, my love, but you had lived so secluded that I felt it to be of the first importance that you should become acquainted with a great many gentlemen before making your choice. And your behaviour has been unexceptionable. You have admirers in plenty, but I venture to swear that not one of them has overstepped the line of what is permissible."

Charmian blushed furiously at the memory of one gentleman who had certainly done so. Lady Cecilia, ascribing this phenomenon to confusion at her words of praise, patted her hand kindly. "And see how well it has answered," she pointed out. "To have attached Stanton Hoborough is a triumph indeed! Not that one can rely upon his making you an offer. With him, of course, all must depend upon his aunt's approval. He will never marry without it, since she would certainly cut him out of her Will."

This pronouncement did nothing to recommend the gentleman to Charmian, and even Lady Cecilia conceded that he lived rather too much in Miss Hoborough's pocket. "It would have been better if he had adopted some profession," she said vaguely, "but there, I daresay she would not have permitted it."

"Fellow's no more than a tame pussy cat," grunted Sir George. "Don't you take him, my girl, even if he *does* offer for you."

Charmian said sedately that she had no immediate thought of marrying any one, and that if Lady Cecilia had no errands for her she would busy herself with neglected correspondence.

"I mean to write to Miss Somersby," she said. "My old schoolmistress. She may be able to advise me about seeking employment. And also to Mama's lawyer to find out just how my affairs stand."

Lady Cecilia exclaimed in dismay. Surely Charmian would make her home at Medhurst? She need not feel herself under any obligation, for her companionship would be a godsend to poor Mary. Nor need she imagine that she would be immured for ever in quiet Medhurst. There would be visits to Town—perhaps even another Season.

Impossible to explain that Medhurst was out of the question. She could only repeat that she had already imposed for far too long on the kindness and hospitality of her new friends. Lady Cecilia said no more, but it was plain that she was sadly disappointed, even hurt. Charmian went off to write her letters feeling miserably guilty and ungrateful.

NINE

IT WAS IMPOSSIBLE TO EVADE A BRIEF farewell to Medhurst. Courtesy and necessity were alike insistent. She must convey to Lady Medhurst something of the delight that she had found in the London scene and try to thank her adequately for promoting the visit. Then there was Susan's future to be discussed. If Susan was happy at Medhurst, perhaps she at least could stay on. Charmian's own plans were no further forward. The replies to her letters had been frustrating. Miss Somersby had written kindly. She would be pleased to recommend her former pupil if she heard of a suitable opening —but at the moment she did not know of one. Mr. Sanbury was sothing but evasive. He thought it would simplify matters if he made up his account when she left Town and promised himself the pleasure of waiting on her at Medhurst to explain her exact financial position. Meanwhile she had no cause for anxiety.

Charmian found that difficult to believe. She began to feel that a number of kindly disposed persons were engaged in trying to shield her from the impact of harsh reality and to manoeuvre her into doing what *they* thought best for her. So it was with mixed feelings that she bade goodbye to Portland Place and set out once more for Medhurst. She was truly grateful for all the kindness that had been showered upon her but she did wish that her benefactors would accept the fact that she was no longer a child and was well able to stand on her own feet.

She found that no one could bear resentment in face of Mary Medhurst's simple affection. From the warmth of her welcome the girl might have been a cherished daughter. She was kissed and patted and held at arm's length while her looks and her travelling dress were carefully appraised, and all the while the soft pretty voice was murmuring its pleasure at her return and launching into eager plans for her entertainment. "And we have given you your own old room," she concluded, taking Charmian's hand to lead her up the stairs, as though she could not consent to lose her company so soon.

It was like being enmeshed by cobwebs, thought Charmian helplessly. How could one disappoint a creature so loving and sincere? So one day drifted into another and still she stayed on, playing the part of daughter of the house to her hostess's great comfort and with only an occasional wry smile for the irony of her situation. Daily she searched the columns of the newspapers in growing desperation. Only by presenting Lady Medhurst with the visual evidence of a post for which she intended to make application could she hope to convince her that her desire for independence remained unshaken. But so far she had sought in vain.

She had been at Medhurst for more than a week when an unexpected visitor arrived. There were so few callers that the two ladies were quite unprepared. They were, in fact, engaged in the homely task of washing a tea service too delicate to be entrusted to less careful hands. When Noakes announced Mr. Hoborough there was a hasty pulling off of borrowed aprons and a setting to rights of ruffled hair before they were able to proceed to the parlour, Lady Medhurst bubbling with delighted curiosity to inspect Charmian's beau, the girl herself a little dismayed. She was a modest creature, but so signal a mark of attention could mean only one thing. Medhurst and Brent Abbas were just too far apart to be on common place calling terms and Lady Medhurst had never so much as set eyes on the handsome gentleman who now came visiting in such friendly fashion.

His excuse was of the flimsiest. Having come across a copy of Mr. Southey's life of Nelson which had reminded him that Merton Place had once housed the Nation's Hero, he had thought that Miss Tracy, living in the vicinity, would certainly wish to read it. He told this unlikely tale with an ingenuous charm that was perhaps a little boyish for his actual years, but he was tall and good-looking and most exquisitely arrayed. And if his manners were a little too polished, a little too caressing for Lady Medhurst's taste, that was because she was accustomed to the more casual ways of her son. A very personable beau indeed, with any number of demure damsels on the catch for him if Cecil was to be believed, though it did not look as though Charmian was one of them, decided Lady Medhurst, noting the cool reserve with which the girl deflected the conversation to impersonal topics.

Perhaps that was what had attracted Mr. Hoborough in the first place. Some men always desired the unattainable. But in Charmian's case she doubted if the air of reserve was just clever strategy. A London season might have taught her to mask her feelings in some degree, but if this confident gentleman had really touched her heart Lady Medhurst thought it would have been plain to see. Still, it was all very intriguing. Cecil had written that he seemed to be very much taken with the child but that all would depend on his formidable aunt. Lady Medhurst liked him the better for pursuing his courtship without waiting for such endorsement.

Moreover, in his attempts to fix his interest with the younger lady, he was by no means neglectful of the older one. He treated her with delightful deference and paid her several delicate compliments. If she had not been old enough to be his mother one might almost have suspected him of initiating a subtle flirtation.

Finally he broached the subject of further visits. They would be coming to the birthday ball, of course, but that was all of three weeks away. Could they not arrange some little outing to bridge the yawning gap between? He would dearly like to explore the pretty countryside through which he had driven today. Would the ladies consent to act as guides? He would be very happy to drive over on the next sunny day and risk the possibility that he might find them otherwise engaged. A pair of fine eyes sought Lady Medhurst's, their message unmistakeable.

One could not possibly repulse so humble and eager a suppliant. The poor man must be fathoms deep in love, thought Lady Medhurst compassionately. Unfortunately Charmian's face showed no answering enthusiasm. Her ladyship said temperately that, while they would naturally be delighted, it seemed a very long way to drive if he were to find them away from home. Mr. Hoborough refused to be discouraged. Brent Abbas, he said, with his charming, deprecatory smile, was no place at the moment for a mere male, seething as it was with preparations for the ball. If he was so unfortunate as to find the ladies from home, at least he would have escaped *that* hurly-burly for a while. And the exercise would be good for the horses. He allowed her no opportunity for further demur, exclaiming that he had already exceeded the conventional twenty minutes, though that was quite Lady Medhurst's blame, so kindly as she had welcomed him, and, on this rather fatuous note, took his leave.

Those horses were very adequately exercised during the weeks that followed. Almost every other day they came trotting up to the door. Charmian began to feel positively hunted and begged Lady Medhurst on no account to desert her during this persistent suitor's visits, so that the poor lady had to feign a quite uncharacteristic stupidity, remaining deaf and blind to hints that grew more and more blatant.

It was a state of affairs that could not last indefinitely. Mr. Hoborough was eventually granted the opportunity that he sought when he arrived at Medhurst on a grey, blustery day of intermittent showers. It was scarcely the day that ladies would choose for driving out, but on this occasion he was the bearer of the formal invitation to his aunt's ball. They discussed the arrangements for this event in some detail. Lady Medhurst, while almost childishly excited at the thought of attending her first grand party in a twelvemonth, was still uneasy at the prospect of deserting her husband for so long. Charmian, setting aside her own doubts, pointed out that there would be both Nan and Susan, as well as the faithful Butterbeck to minister to his lordship's needs. Surely his wife could confidently resign him to their devoted care? Moreover, of late, his condition had steadily improved.

Her ladyship was just explaining that it was this very circumstance, with the consequent determination that there should be no set-back caused by *her* negligence, that made her anxious, when fate took a hand in the argument. Noakes came in to inform her that Sir William Knighton had called. Finding himself in the neighbourhood on a professional matter, he had ventured to hope that she would not object to it if he came—quite *un*professionally, he assured her, with his charming smile—to enquire how his lordship was going on.

Lady Medhurst, who valued Sir William for his kindness and his unassuming manners almost as much as for his skill, exclaimed that no visitor could be more welcome. He must come at once and see for himself how well the patient was progressing. Forgetful of everything else, she flitted out of the room ahead of him, all eager delight.

"Encroaching sort of fellow," said Mr. Hoborough sourly. "One would think him a man of rank, calling upon ladies because he 'chanced' to be in the neighbourhood forsooth. Well—he may be physician to the Prince Regent, but when all's said and done he's naught but an apothecary. Very unwise to be treating him as an equal. Such people have no notion of keeping the line and are all too easily puffed up with an inflated notion of their own consequence."

Charmian could only stare in amazement. She knew the high regard in which Sir William was held, both by Sir George and Lady Cecilia and by other members of their circle. On the one or two occasions that she had met him socially she had liked him. He seemed to be able to inspire confidence in his patients, too, and she had felt that she would think herself fortunate—should the need ever arise—to secure the services of so kindly and competent a medical adviser.

But before she could draw breath to speak in his defence, Mr. Hoborough was off on a different tack. Favouring her with his most charming smile he went on, "However, today at least he has earned my gratitude by detaching your damnably persistent duenna. The wretched woman might have thought me bent upon seduction, so close as she has kept you, but you, my dear Miss Tracy, can be under no misapprehension. You must have realised that I have only been awaiting a suitable opportunity to declare myself in form. It is my earnest desire to make you my wife."

A swift, sidelong glance at Charmian's face did nothing to encourage his hopes and caused him to press on before she could reject him out of hand.

"You will say it is too soon—that we are not well enough acquainted. But if you will permit me to explain, I am rather awkwardly situated." He hesitated briefly as though choosing his words, then went on, "I am well aware of what is said of me. No doubt it has been said in your hearing—that I hang upon my aunt's sleeve and would never marry to displease her. I will not deny that there is a good deal of truth in the charge. My father was killed when I was no more than a babe and my mother married again and consigned me to Aunt Tabitha's care. My paternal inheritance is meagre but my aunt has always been extremely generous and for that I owe her both gratitude and loyalty and would not willingly displease her. In the matter of my marriage, however, I reserve the right to make my own choice, and this I was anxious that you should know. Perhaps I have been too precipitate. Better that than have you believe that I proposed to you at my aunt's behest."

It was soberly, simply said. If Charmian had felt any affection for him she would doubtless have been duly touched. As it was she could not wholly forget the unpleasant impression left by his attitude to Sir William and his spiteful references to Lady Medhurst. She said quietly, "I appreciate the delicacy of your position, sir, and thank you for your candour." Then she, in her turn, hesitated. One could scarcely enquire how, in the circumstances he had described, he proposed to support a wife! Was she, too, to be dependent on Miss Hoborough's bounty? If so, small wonder that the lady expected to be consulted.

She said formally, "I am truly appreciative of the honour that you do me, sir, but I feel myself obliged to decline." And then, more carefully, "We should not suit, you know. *You* are a leading figure in the world of fashion and your wife must be able to take her place at your side—an accomplished hostess, conversant with all the nice distinctions that will for ever be a mystery to me. I should be wholly inadequate to the exacting demands of such a position, and, to be frank, an existence entirely devoted to entertaining and being entertained would very soon bore me to extinction. So let us part friends, sir, and since, as you said, our acquaintance is but brief, I trust that you will soon forget that you ever cherished a fancy for making me your wife."

The calm common sense of her reply gave Mr. Hoborough the opportunity to withdraw with dignity. He did not avail himself of it. He even smiled a little as he told her kindly, "Your modesty is one of the traits that I have much admired in your disposition. Pray believe me when I say that with my guidance and support you could fill such a position to admiration. And I know what I am speaking of. As for boredom—No, my love, I would see to it that you should not be bored. You are young and quite untaught. It would be my privilege and pleasure to forward your education in so many ways. And then there would be our children, you know. Indeed you must see that your life would be full and interesting. But, as I feared, I have been too precipitate. I shall hope to receive a more favourable answer when you have had time to think things over, and will even promise not to tease you too soon with further appeals now that you know my mind in the matter."

This calm assumption of superior wisdom made Charmian seethe with fury. Fortunately, before she could express her unflattering opinion of pompous, patronising prigs, Lady Medhurst came back, obviously happy in the doctor's opinion of her husband's progress and full of apologies for having abandoned and neglected her other guest—which made Charmian crosser than ever.

"Though I daresay you entertained each other very well without me," she ended, mischievous in her high spirits.

He bowed. "Yes, indeed, ma'am. Now I must crave your indulgence if I do not visit you for several days. Arrangements have now reached the point at which I can be of assistance to my aunt. But I promise that I shall not fail to drive over and give you safe escort to Brent Abbas."

In her present mood Lady Medhurst was happily impervious to ominous overtones. "Indeed you must not dream of putting yourself to such pains, Mr. Hoborough," she exclaimed cheerfully. "Sir William has just told me that my nephew has come home on furlough at last. Depend upon it that I shall hear from Cecilia by tomorrow or the next day at latest that they mean to descend on Medhurst in time to attend the ball. Jasper is a great favourite with your aunt, you know. She will certainly wish to include him among her guests when she knows that he is staying with us. You will like him," she turned to Charmian. "He is so good humoured and easygoing. I daresay he will try to flirt with you because you are so pretty, but it is all funning. Just high spirits, you know, because he is free for a while from his regimental duties."

It seemed that Mr. Hoborough did not share his aunt's partiality for military gentlemen. "No doubt his high spirits prevent him from giving a thought to the expectations that he has aroused," he said waspishly. "Though if a female is so foolish as to succumb to the glamour of regimentals, I daresay it is no more than she deserves."

The blank astonishment on Lady Medhurst's face gave way to strong displeasure. "My nephew is a gentleman," she said icily. "He would never arouse expectations that he had no intention of fulfilling. And my remarks were not addressed to you."

Mr. Hoborough had already realised his error. He made a valiant attempt to recover lost ground. "Forgive me, ma'am," he begged. " 'Twas disappointment and, I confess, jealousy that made me speak so intemperately. I had counted on having the pleasure of being your escort and it is hard to have to yield it to another, be he never so much your nephew."

The fine eyes were beseeching, the whole pose expressed deep penitence and humble admiration. But Lady Medhurst was not appeased. Instinctively she distrusted such attitudinising and felt that the earlier caustic comments were probably much more representative of the gentleman's real disposition. She said coolly, "Very well. We will not refine further on so trivial a matter. And since there is much to do in preparing for my guests, I will bid you good day."

TEN

MATTERS FELL OUT MUCH AS LADY MED-
hurst had anticipated, save that it was not a letter
that brought news of visitors, but nephew Jasper
himself. After a week of idleness and tolerant sub-
mission to his mother's cossetting, that young gentleman felt the need of exercise to release his abundant
energy. He also harboured a mild curiosity about
this Miss Tracy who figured so prominently in
Mama's accounts of her recent activities, a sentiment fostered by the comments of one or two of his
cronies who openly envied him the privilege of domestic association with the lady. Naturally he did
not undeceive them, promptly adopting the proprietary airs of one who had been on easy terms with the
lady since nursery days. In fact he was not much in
the petticoat line—no more than was necessary to
assert his freedom from apron strings—but it occurred to him that it would be as well to be able to

recognise the chit if they chanced to meet in some public place.

And Charmian did indeed like him. He was about her own age, a carefree kindly young man, not particularly good looking, though he had a well-knit athletic figure and carried himself with the easy arrogance that she had come to recognise as the mark of the military man. From the outset she felt comfortable with him as she had never been with Mr. Hoborough, and before he went back to Town they had gone far towards substantiating his pretence of close acquaintance. They had caught up on the 'cradle days' legend as they compared childish likes and dislikes and agreed that boys' schools were probably more detestable than girls' though both were bad. Charmian had been properly impressed by the traveller's tales and carefully expurgated military anecdotes produced for her entertainment, and Jasper, if his heart was touched by her forlorn history—which he had already heard from his Mama—had the instictive tact to mask his pity with a flow of laughing nonsense, suggesting several highly improbable tales to account for her appearance in that snow-bound mail coach. Finally they spent a hilarious hour over dinner, discussing with Lady Medhurst the enthralling topic of costumes suitable for the ball. Jasper, of course, had no problem. As he pointed out, fashions in regimentals did not change appreciably in a mere thirty years.

"I daresay it has something to do with the masculine preference for comfort," he told them seriously. "We men prefer to keep our waist-lines in the place that nature intended."

His aunt promptly demolished this argument, declaring that men had no notion of comfort so far as dress was concerned. "Vain as peacocks, all of you," she asserted, "and soldiers the worst of all. While if you mean to tell me that skin-tight inexpressibles, a coat that must be coaxed over your shoulders and a neckcloth a foot high, so stiffly starched that you may cut yourself on it if you turn your head sharply, are your notion of comfort," she told him, running a knowledgeable eye over his comfortable riding clothes, "I shall say you are a candidate for Bedlam."

Jasper glanced down affectionately at his old coat. The afternoon had passed so swiftly that he had been persuaded to stay and dine with them before he remembered that he would be obliged to sit down to table most inappropriately dressed.

"But my dear aunt! My very dear aunt!" he said in an affected drawl. "One *does* not turn one's head sharply. Or make *any* impulsive ill-regulated movements. Shocking bad *ton*! One preserves at all times a bored if slightly vacuous front, with no show of emotion in face of either disaster or delight. So the high stock, you see, is quite essential. It positively *prevents* a fellow from transgressing the code of proper conduct."

He shook his head sadly over their irreverent

laughter at this faithful sketch of the bearing of a man of fashion and relapsed into his natural manner, promising that he would be with them again before the week was out and enquiring if there was anything that he could bring them from Town. His aunt mentioned one or two items that his mother could obtain for her, but Charmian, so newly come from London, wanted nothing.

Together they waved him away in the gentle light of the quarter moon. Her ladyship smiled triumphantly at Charmian. "Well?" she demanded.

The girl smiled back. "Yes, indeed," she agreed promptly. "A delightful young man, and just as you described him. I met no one in Town whom I like half so well. Do you suppose it is because his life is so full and absorbing? He has no time to think about his appearance or the effect he is making and so is just his natural likeable self."

They debated this theory idly as they turned back to the house, Lady Medhurst going so far as to say that, in marked contrast to her nephew, Mr. Hoborough gave one the impression that his every pose and gesture had been carefully rehearsed in front of a mirror.

They were now fully occupied in making the house ready for the guests. Rooms might be shabby but they could be scrubbed and polished until they gleamed with cleanliness. Linen must be aired and silver brought out from the strong box. Careful planning must provide for tempting and varied meals without undue extravagance. Lady Medhurst was inclined to shy at this last limitation. Guests, she felt, should have the best of everything whatever the cost. Charmian worked on her patiently. Any one, she suggested, could produce a satisfactory result by using costly ingredients. The really talented housekeeper produced something unusual to surprise and intrigue her guests. Let Susan confer with the cook and see if they could adapt some of those mouth-watering Virginian recipes with which she loved to confound Nan. Lady Medhurst consented rather doubtfully, but somehow most of the catering arrangements devolved on Charmian, her hostess reflecting comfortably that since, in any case, the wines would be above reproach, the gentlemen would not be unduly critical. As for Cecil, she was always a finicky eater. Careful of her figure of course. Her ladyship smiled rather smugly, smoothing her skirts over hips that were still neat without any such self-denial.

Even in the apartments of the invalid there was a new ripple of life. His lordship, Butterbeck told Charmian confidentially, was eager to hear the details of Quatre Bras at first hand from his nephew. He was even hopeful of being well enough to come downstairs. Sir William had agreed that he might do so if he felt able.

In all this bustle there was little time to think of ball costumes. It was not until the guests were comfortably installed that they were able to devote themselves to such frivolous matters. It had already been agreed that Charmian should wear the bronze-gold taffeta that she had borrowed on her first night at Medhurst, and Lady Cecilia had brought with her an elegant costume especially made for the occasion so that they were able to concentrate on the provision of a becoming gown for Lady Med-hurst. They eventually contrived a delightful polo-naise effect, using one of her own dresses for the under-gown and making the overdress from breadths of silk cut from an old bed curtain that they found laid away in the attic.

On the evening of the ball Charmian dressed early so that there would be plenty of time for Nan to arrange her hair before she was needed to attend on her mistress. Despite the prospect of an eve-ning's pleasuring that, six months ago, would have set her ablaze with eager anticipation, she was in low spirits. The thought of meeting her rejected suitor did nothing to mend this, the less so because she knew that he had not fully accepted her rejec-tion. And though the obligations of a hostess might prevent Miss Hoborough from questioning one insig-nificant girl, she could not feel entirely easy on this head. It was all very well for the older ladies to insist that none of them had lied. They had only withheld certain parts of the truth, and it really did not matter very much if these must now be disclosed. Charmian had never felt happy about this paltering with truth, and Mr. Hoborough's offer of marriage had deepened her discomfort. She was sure that it would never have been made if he had not thought her related to the Medhursts; well-connected if not necessarily well-dowered. For of one thing she was convinced. He was not in the least in love with her. Her acquaintance with love might have been all too fleeting, but it had taught her to distinguish true metal from counterfeit.

So she came to the underlying cause of her low spirits. Perhaps it was wearing the gown that had earned Rolf's commendation that brought it home to her as nothing else could. Try as she would, she found herself quite unable to forget those moments in the library at Portland Place. The more she tried to bury them in forgetfulness or busy-ness, the more insistent they became. The truth was staring her in the face at last. If only it was Rolf who was taking her to the ball! Of all the men she had met during those months in Town, of the several who had paid court to her, he, alone, who had met her with antagonism and yet had somehow become her counsellor and comforter, was the one who had touched her heart. And it was all so hopeless. Sadly she wondered if, among his many preoccupations, he ever remembered that brief, rapturous interlude.

A fine mood in which to start the evening, she told herself crossly, and, on sudden impulse, picked up the little coffer in which she kept her modest trinkets. Tonight she would wear her own special Charmian amulet. It might bring her good fortune.

She never *had* worn it and it did not really go with this dress, but she had a sudden fancy to do so. She fastened the well-worn chain about her throat, smiling at the realisation that the low décolletage no longer abashed her, blew out the candles and went downstairs.

The hall was deserted. Everyone else was dressing for the party. But since the evening was chilly, there was a fire glowing gently in the great stone hearth, and instinctively she responded to its invitation, gazing down pensively into the little flickering flames, one hand idly fingering her locket. She wondered, childishly, if it could grant her a wish, like the magical talismans in fairy tales.

The front door opened briskly. A gentleman in a driving coat that sported only three modest capes strode confidently into the hall, tossing his hat and gloves on to a table already littered with similar impedimenta and shrugging himself out of his coat before he noticed the lady standing on the hearth. When he did so his face lit to delight and he crossed the space that divided them in half a dozen swift strides, to catch her against his breast and say eagerly, breathlessly, "Charmian! Sweetheart! I *had* to come."

With which he stooped and kissed her, a comprehensive exercise which lasted some time and did all that was required to raise the recipient's spirits.

Presently he raised his head, still holding her close as though he feared she might vanish, and said rather lamely, "I had to see if it was still the same for you. And it is, isn't it, beloved? Try as I will—and I *have* tried—I cannot put you out of my mind. Will you marry me—now? Be poor with me, just so that we can be together."

She nodded eagerly, breathed, "Oh! Yes please!" on a worshipful note, and was kissed again, rather more gently. He smiled down at her ruefully and said, "I am well aware that I should not have asked it of you but it is quite your own fault, you know. You seem to have the most devastating effect on the principles in which I was bred. From our very first meeting, when I greeted you with less than courtesy, my behaviour has steadily deteriorated. And to be asking you to marry me now, when my fortunes are at such low ebb, is quite shameful. Only I found I *could* not stand by and let some other man steal you from me. Some other man who could not possibly love you as much as I do. Though it's little enough save love that I can offer. We shall probably have to let Medhurst go eventually, though I have reasonable hopes of making a modest success of Ryelands. A gentleman of honour, if he spoke at all, would ask you to wait until that success was assured. Very well—I am not such a man. But at least I'll not deceive you. As matters stand as present I can support you in reasonable comfort. But there will be no Town house or smart carriage, no extravagant parties, no jewels, not even very many pretty dresses."

"Just you," nodded Charmian.

"Just me," he agreed soberly. "Needing your love, your understanding, your encouragement, as I need the air I breathe. Will you still accept me on those terms?"

Something fierce and primitive within her leapt to life at his words. She gloried in the challenge, knew that she could meet his need and find happiness in doing so. But her voice was quiet and composed as he said gently, "Accept you? Yes. Proudly —humbly—gratefully. Do you not see? You offer me something far beyond material benefits. For the first time in my life I am really wanted. I shall have a place where I belong—in your heart—and a name which is truly mine."

Mr. Heriot was of the opinion that the place where she belonged at that moment was in his arms, so that he could the more conveniently express his approval of her sentiments, but they were not granted much time to dally in their private paradise. Overhead there were sounds of activity. A door slammed. There were footsteps, a laughing exclamation, the murmur of conversation.

Charmian said swiftly, shyly, "Don't tell them yet. Please!"

He smiled at her—ready in that moment to gratify any wish that she might express—and said understandingly, "Of course not. In all the bustle of setting out for Godmama's party? And I must make haste to change or I shall be quite shockingly late. You will save a dance for me? Or two? And supper, perhaps? Tomorrow we will tell them our news."

He snatched a last fleeting kiss and turned to greet his mother who came hurrying in exclaiming her delight and surprise at his unexpected arrival and fretting that she had not made due preparation.

"Why—I grew weary of brooding over sodden meadows," he told her lightly. "As for preparation —if you will have one of the maids press out those duds of Granpapa's, I shall manage very well. You are not to be waiting for me. Present my apologies for tardiness to my godmother and assure her that I will make what speed I may."

He took the stairs two at a time, swerving to avoid a collision with a magnificently accoutred Jasper, who had just emerged from his room, and calling a laughing insult over his shoulder in reply to that gentleman's startled oath.

"Dear boy!" said his Mama fondly. "It is good to see him in spirits," and turned her attention to Charmian's appearance.

Their overnight gear had been despatched in the gig earlier in the day, so they were able to set out without further delay. Only the three ladies were to stay the night, Jasper having thankfully accepted Miss Hoborough's decision that she was unequal to the task of entertaining male house guests when all her energies were absorbed by the ball. He made light of the toilsome double journey, confiding to Charmian that Miss Hoborough terrified him, despite her professed penchant for his society, and that he had far rather make the journey *four* times than run the risk of the raking down he might get if she chanced to be out of humour next day. But it *was* a long drive, even though the weather had chosen to acknowledge the importance of the birthday ball and the moon shone serenely from unclouded skies. Remembering how many times Mr. Hoborough had driven over to visit her, Charmian felt quite certain qualms of conscience. Perhaps, in his cool sardonic fashion, he had cared for her more than she had guessed. Why else should he have put himself to such trouble?

Brent Abbas was very old, very lovely. Set in its dark filigree of trees it lay placidly—almost smugly —a-sprawl in the moonlight, awaiting their admiration. But there was little time to pay homage to its perfection. Miss Hoborough, a hostess of the old school, greeted her guests as they crossed her threshold, in a vaulted hall that boasted two enormous hearths with hooded canopies. There were no imposing coats of arms, no ostentatious marks of pedigree. Only the stones themselves proclaimed their ancient lineage. Impellingly one's gaze was led to the carved bosses that adorned the room-rib overhead. But Miss Hoborough was graciously expressing her pleasure in their coming, adding—a little more genially—

her satisfaction at the prospect of her godson's attendance, and, as other guests followed hard on their heels, suggesting that the ladies would like to lay aside their cloaks and prink a little, and that they would find Marjie in attendance in the oriel room.

"No state occasion at Brent Abbas would be complete without Marjie," explained Lady Medhurst, as they followed Lady Cecilia up the steps that led to this apartment. "She has served the Hoboroughs all her days. She is quite incredibly old. I believe she was actually Miss Hoborough's nurse—and perfectly convinced that nothing can be managed properly without her oversight."

Marjie was a tiny creature, even shorter than Charmian, and so shrivelled and faded that one felt she might drift away like a dried leaf. But her eyes were still bright and alert and she smoothed Lady Cecilia's luxurious mantle lovingly as she folded it. Charmian put off her own cloak and turned to the mirror that had been set up for the convenience of the guests, coaxing an errant curl into place with practised fingers.

Over her shoulder she could see Marjie's reflection as the old woman took Lady Medhurst's wrap and laid it tidily beside her sister's, and then turned to see if *she* needed any assistance. Through the mirror she smiled an acknowledgement and slightly shook her head.

There was a choking gasp. Amazement? Fear? Marjie put up trembling hands to her mouth and quavered, "Miss Charmian!" And as one only half believing, "Lord have mercy! 'Tis a spirit I'm seeing. After all the long years. Miss Charmian!"

ELEVEN

BUT DESPITE HER AIR OF FRAGILITY, MAR-
jie was made of tough fibre. Coaxed into a chair
by Lady Cecilia and stimulated by a refreshing
sniff at Lady Medhurst's vinaigrette, her agitation
soon subsided, and the realisation that the young
lady who had so startled her was no ghostly appari-
tion but very much warm flesh and blood exerted
a powerful restorative effect.

"Our Miss Charmian's daughter?" she asked
tentatively. And when there was no immediate
response, answered her own question. "Of course
you are, whether you know it or not, and you her
very image. 'Sides—that's her locket you're wearing—the one Misss Tabitha gave her. I'd know it
anywhere. Has her name scratched on it, too, the
naughty little imp, when she made up her mind
that she wouldn't be called Dorcas any more. Said
it sounded like a hen squawking, and in future we
was all to call her by the pretty name she'd picked

out for herself. Just eight years old she was, and *that* determined! Got her own way in the end— wouldn't answer to anything else, even from her Papa, for all the whippings she got, and Miss Tabitha just doting on her and gaving way to her whims. Spoiled her to death, I s'pose, and just about broke her heart when she ran off the way she did. But here am I gabbing on and work to be done," she ended abruptly, as a new party of guests could be heard approaching. She got up, hesitated a moment, and then said, on a note nicely pitched between command and supplication, "Don't tell Miss Tabitha. Not yet. She's not able to see for herself, poor lady, and a few hours more'll not hurt, not after the years she's sought you and mourned you as lost. And to come on her birthday! What a blessed thing! I'm fain to be by when you tell her—but she'd choose to hear it quietly when all the company has gone." She turned to address Charmian directly. "Please," she finished simply. And Charmian, burning with eagerness to hear the rest of the half-told tale, found herself pressing the wrinkled hand and agreeing that Marjie's way was best.

"As indeed it is," pronounced Lady Cecilia with elder-sisterly firmness, as the three made their way to the ballroom. "I *do* vaguely remember some tale about a younger Hoborough girl. But it is so long ago that I cannot recall the details. I rather think there was a runaway match, before she was even 'out'. *Not* the kind of story that one wishes to resurrect with half the 'ton' listening."

Six months ago Charmian would not have believed that Marjie's recognition could seem relatively unimportant. To be sure she was excited and intrigued, but with the prospect of dancing with Rolf to occupy her thoughts it was surprisingly easy to push further speculation aside. And in fact she enjoyed a delightful evening. The old-world costumes of the guests gave it something of dream-like atmosphere that was exactly suited to her present mood. She received several compliments on her appearance, was besieged by partners and, in her new-born happiness and confidence, was even able to shrug off the embarrassing particularity of Mr. Hoborough's attentions. That gentleman's air was proprietary to say the least, and gave cause for several of the guests to exchange knowing glances and understanding nods. Moreover Jasper, sizing up the situation with delight, chose to pay extravagant court to her, at which Mr. Hoborough drew a sour mouth and actually took it upon himself to suggest that, as 'that mountebank's antics' were attracting undesirable attention, it would be better if she did not grant him a second dance.

For a moment the issue hung in the balance. Only the belated arrival of Mr. Heriot saved Mr. Hoborough from a withering set-down.

It commanded her whole attention. The grandfather whose clothes Rolf wore—that same Lord

Medhurst of whom Susan had spoken with such awed respect—must have been a man of very similar build, for the full-skirted coat, the long, embroidered waistcoat and satin small-clothes fitted his grandson to a nicety. Unlike most of the male guests, he carried his brocades and silks with that same indifferent ease with which he shrugged himself into his shabby workaday clothes. The wig made him look a little different, its whiteness, matching the foaming lace of his cravat, contrasting strongly with his weather-browned skin. Charmian was too young to know that the beautiful lace should have been enriched by the glitter of diamonds, the slender fingers that raised the quizzing glass in mock disapproval of Jasper's pretensions have been loaded with costly rings. She only knew that he looked magnificent, and that she adored him. The remainder of the evening passed in a happy, dreaming daze. She did not even bestir herself to tell him of Marjie's recognition. In any case there was little opportunity. The dances that she had saved for him seemed to be over so quickly and at supper they were joined by Jasper and his partner. It was not until the party was over and she had bidden Rolf a reluctant and extremely correct goodnight that her thoughts returned to her own affairs and she wondered if the time had come for further revelations. Perhaps Miss Hoborough would be exhausted and would wish to retire at once. Her attentive nephew was fussing over her with offers of refreshment, declaring that she had eaten nothing all evening, so busy as she had been in seeing to the comfort of others. She eyed him with tolerant amusement.

"My dear boy, on occasions such as this I always have a tray in my room before I dress, knowing that there will be no opportunity of eating later. In any case I do not care for all these kickshaws"— thus dismissing an array that would be the talk of the countryside for days and that had aroused bitter envy in the breasts of several prominent hostesses who had been privileged to partake of it. "No do I need a footstool," she went on, a shade impatiently. "If you wish to be of use, ask Marjie to make us a bowl of negus. You will like that, won't you?" she suggested to the two older ladies. "Some hot milk for the child, I suppose. Though my negus won't hurt her. It's mild enough, but we'll all sleep the better for it. Marjie makes it just as I like it—the lemon and spice exactly right. And then we women folk can enjoy a comfortable coze. I can never sleep immediately after such a party as this. My mind is wide awake however weary my body may be."

Charmian having chosen to drink negus with her elders, Mr. Hoborough went off on his errand. The ladies chatted in desultory fashion, the guests expressing their appreciation of the evening's festivities and Charmian begging permission to examine the tapestries with which the room was hung and wondering if she was, in fact, surveying the home of her ancestors.

Marjie, coming in with the negus, caught Lady Cecilia's eye and nodded. She set down the tray and began to ladle the steaming brew into the heavy glasses. Lady Cecilia said slowly, "Marjie has something to tell you, ma'am. Something that she noticed as soon as we arrived tonight."

Their hostess's face expressed mild interest. She held out a hand for her glass. "Indeed?" she enquired pleasantly.

Marjie said bluntly, "It's the young lady, ma'am. Miss Tracy. How she came by *that* name I'd not be knowing, but she's the very image of our Miss Charmian and I'd stake my life on it she's her daughter. What's more she's wearing Miss Charmian's silver locket that *you* gave her. If you was to look at the back of it, I'll lay you'd still find her name scratched there."

She faltered into sudden silence, abashed by her own reference to 'looking'. Poor Miss Tabitha! Who could neither read the testimony writ so plain in the girl's face nor peer at the scratches on an old trinket, but must rely on the reports of others. She said in more subdued fashion, "Perhaps the ladies can tell you the full tale of it, ma'am. I just wanted you to know that this is none of their doing. 'Twas I that recognised the likeness."

Miss Hoborough's complexion was naturally pale. She did not change colour nor exclaim. Only she set down her untouched glass and leaned forward in her chair with that painful, peering attitude, as though by sheer determination she would force herself to see. Presently she said slowly, heavily, "I knew there was some mystery when you were presented to me as a Miss Tracy who claimed to be a connection of the Medhursts. Now it would appear that you also claim relationship with me. I may not see very well, Miss Tracy, but I am not easily deceived. Since Marjie seems to have been struck by a resemblance that I am unable to estimate, I will listen to your story—but it had better be the truth."

For a moment Charmian was very angry. Miss Hoborough was as odious as her nephew and she had no desire to claim kinship with either. Only the timely recollection that Miss Hoborough was her hostess and that she also owed a debt of gratitude to her kindly sponsors, who were looking distinctly anxious, enabled her to reply with some degree of moderation. She swallowed the hasty words that scorched her tongue-tip but could not wholly quell the note of indignation as she said, "It will not take long, ma'am. The truth is that I make no claim and that I have no story."

Miss Hoborough's hands, tightly clenched on the fan in her lap, slowly relaxed. A reluctant smile softened the grim line of her mouth. "Good girl," she said, and her voice sounded almost amused. "Good blood, any way, wherever it came from.

Perhaps you will be so kind as to tell me how you come to be called Tracy."

"Yes, do explain, Charmian," interposed Mary Medhurst eagerly. "You cannot expect her to understand when she knows nothing of the circumstances."

"Charmian," repeated Miss Hoborough thoughtfully. "Have you always been called Charmian, child?"

"For as long as I can remember. That is a point that you could easily verify by enquiry in Wivelsfield or at the school which I attended. And means nothing. As for Tracy—I was adopted in infancy by a Mrs. Tracy, who gave me her name, since I had none of my own."

"Charmian, you are being very naughty," pronounced Lady Cecilia severely. "Anyone would think you did not *wish* to trace your family. With your permission"—she did not wait for it—"I will tell the story myself."

Miss Hoborough listened in silence. At the end she said sharply, "And the Medhurst connection?"

This time it was Mary Medhurst who answered. "Mrs. Tracy was the unfortunate American lady with whom Philip, thinking himself free to do so, had gone through a form of marriage."

"But the girl is not the child of that union?"

"There *was* a child—a little girl," said Charmian quietly, her anger dying. "Melanie. But she died some time before I was left on Mama's hands. Susan can vouch for that—or Mr. Sanbury, I suppose."

Miss Hoborough got up and took two or three aimless steps about the room. Words that were almost a groan were forced from her. "If only I could see for myself. I would know at once. But I have sought so long—poured out a fortune on the search—even sent Stanton over to France during that uneasy peace at the turn of the century, all to no avail. He brought back a good deal of information. My sister had died of a fever on her husband's Brittany estate. So much was sure. Louis' parents perished in the Terror. His brother, too. But Louis himself had vanished and so had the child, and no trace could be found of either. There were rumours that Louis had thrown in his lot with the new regime and had died in battle, fighting for Buonaparte. It would not surprise me, knowing the views he had held. But where was my niece? Papa had severed all communication with Charmian—*my* Charmian—when she eloped with Louis. Papa was very good at casting people out."

She broke off, pausing in her restless wanderings to finger a fine Minton vase and to sniff absentmindedly at the chrysanthemums that filled another. No one ventured to speak.

Presently she sighed deeply. "So many things fit. Despite Papa's edict I had kept in touch with my sister, and had repeatedly begged her to come home, or at least, to send the child to safety. The woman you describe as being in charge of the baby might well be the 'Gwenny' she wrote of, who shared in her brothers' smuggling trips across the channel. She sounds just such a rough, great-hearted Amazon. But how can I be sure? When one is young it is easy to believe what one wishes to believe. I am old and cynical—a doubting Thomas—and I want proof—incontrovertible proof."

They seemed to have reached an impasse. Charmian thought it probable that Miss Hoborough was indeed her aunt. It no longer seemed particularly important, though she was sorry for the doubt and confusion into which the poor lady was cast. After all, if she had grown resigned to the loss of her niece, would it not have been kinder to let the matter rest? She was thankful that it was not she who had initiated the disclosure.

But Marjie was not prepared to give up so easily. "Begging your pardon, ma'am, but there's the locket, too," she reminded her mistress.

"Ah, yes. The locket," agreed Miss Hoborough almost absently, half smiling for the memories that the locket recalled. Then, suddenly, "If it is *my* Charmian's locket, it may still hold the curls we put into it when I gave it to her." She held out her hand eagerly. "May I see for myself, child?"

Charmian was more disappointed than she had thought to be. She put the locket into her hostess's hand and said regretfully, "I'm sorry, ma'am. It cannot be the same locket, for mine does not open."

The slight fingers, so frail that they seemed almost transparent, turned the locket about carefully.

"Are you quite sure of that?" asked Miss Hoborough.

She twisted the tiny ring that carried the chain and pressed it firmly. The locket sprang open, and something soft and white fluttered out, to be snatched up by the attentive Marjie. Not curls, but a scrap of fine paper, folded very small.

TWELVE

THE FIRST GLIMMER OF DAWN WAS AL-
ready lightening the horizon before the ladies sought
their beds. Marjie had wept over the few feebly
scrawled lines as she read them aloud to her mistress. Already sick of the fever which was to prove
fatal, alone among servants whom she felt to be
inimical and terrified for her baby's safety, the
young mother had taken the desperate step of confiding the child to Cornish Gwenny, the smuggler
lass. The elder sister already knew something of
the isolation in which the younger one had existed,
and of her growing unhappiness. At first it had not
seemed so important that Louis' parents were
deeply displeased by his marriage. They would be
reconciled in time when they saw how happy their
son was. But the discovery that the bride was not
only English and a Protestant but penniless as well,
since Papa had cut her out of his Will, had hardened
disapproval into bitter enmity. There had even been

166

talk of an annulment, but *that* at least Louis had resolutely resisted. His wife was already enceinte. Rather than submit to parental dictates in such a matter, he would abjure his native land and carry his little family to the Americas.

The times were anxious. Louis was an unimportant younger son. The Comte yielded. But that was when a shame-faced Louis escorted a wife already suffering the discomforts of early pregnancy on a tedious and comfortless journey to the most distant and poverty-ridden of his father's estates. It was virtual exile, but the girl-wife had been thankful to go. And at first, life in Brittany had been comparatively pleasant and peaceful. In later pregnancy she had been well—placid, untouched by the ferment that was convulsing France. She had her beloved Louis all to herself. Her letters to her sister were cheerful. She missed her very much, but the total lack of congenial neighbours in her new home did not distress her at all. She could not, in any case, have entertained them in *her* condition. She sewed tranquilly for her baby and did her best to support her husband in his efforts to ease the lot of his father's tenants. Poor Louis! Centuries of oppression could not be wiped out by a few months of just and kindly treatment. His generosity, his friendly overtures, were taken for weakness—even fear. But on the surface all was smooth, and the little Charmian Louise made her appearance in due time, a normal healthy baby.

But once his wife was safely delivered and his conjugal anxieties allayed, Louis grew restless. The news that reached them so tardily from Paris was more and more alarming. Since the abortive flight to Varennes, the king was virtually a prisoner and many of the nobility had fled into voluntary exile. He should not be lingering here in sheltered idleness, he told his wife, when every moderate man was needed to bring the extremists of both sides to some sort of compromise. In this remote spot, Charmian and the child would be quite safe. For himself, his duty was plain.

A few letters came from him at irregular intervals, letters filled with the gloomiest forebodings. Then rumours of sickness among the peasantry reminded his wife of *her* duties. In her husband's absence it became her responsibility to see that necessary medicines were provided and to relieve urgent want. It was a daunting task and she set out rather nervously. She had a tolerably good command of French, but the local patois was a very different matter. And when she reached the village it appeared to be deserted. She knocked on several doors but no one answered. Finally, in desperation she tried the door of one dwelling—one could not call them cottages—and when it opened under her hand, called out to enquire if there was sickness here and if help was needed. A burst of cackling laughter was the only answer, but there was something other than laughter in the face of the woman who presently emerged from the gloom, a famine-thin child clutched to her breast with one arm while with her free hand she made to close the half open door. It was a mask of fanatical hatred; and a repetition of the visitor's enquiry provoked an outburst of vituperation that no patois could disguise.

Charmian shrank back appalled. The door slammed in her face, and from within there came again the muffled sound of maniac laughter.

She had always disliked visiting the village, a mean, sordid place, its tumbledown hovels set in a rough square about the communal well, with scrawny fowls pecking about the unsavoury heaps of rotting refuse that littered the bare-trodden ground, but she had never been frightened before. Today she was aware of a brooding menace. The silent, shuttered dwellings were like so many snarling beasts, crouching to spring. Instinct urged her to run, but her own stubborn courage and an innate sense of the behaviour due to her husband's rank held her back. She would not even turn and retrace her steps, determining to go on across the square and make her way back to the chateau by a rough track that followed the coast. Fervently she wished that she had brought a servant with her. But she had left the only maid whom she liked and trusted to care for her baby. As for the men servants they were a surly, uncouth lot, indifferent or rebellious. And some of the younger ones eyed her with a sly lechery that even her young innocence recognised.

She walked on, head high, the sound of her own pulse beat thundering in her ears.

She was just beyond the last straggling houses when the first clod of earth was flung. It struck her on the shoulder, spattering her dress with mud but doing her no other injury. Several more followed sporadically, most of them falling short. But presently one, better aimed, caught her on the temple. And since it had a sizeable stone embedded in it, it stunned her briefly and stretched her on the rough ground. As she struggled back to consciousness she was aware of two things—the pain in her head and the sight of a woman running towards her from the village. She struggled to her feet, sick and giddy, fearing a further assault, but the newcomer, a tall, strapping wench, cried out to her in English to wait, adding breathlessly that she had come to help, not hurt.

That was her first meeting with Cornish Gwenny. And compassion on one side and gratitude on the other bridged the gap between the strangely assorted pair. A queer kind of alliance sprang up between them. Gwenny feared no man. Her comings and goings were erratic—she made no secret of her connection with the smugglers—but she marched determinedly up to the chateau whenever opportunity offered and demanded speech with the young mistress. In fact she did a good deal, quite unknown to her protegée, to hold together the crumbling feudal authority which alone kept the girl and her baby safe from attack. And it was to Gwenny, to Gwenny arriving late one night with the shocking news of the execution of the king, insisting that now there would be no safety for any one with claims to noble blood, that a distraught and feverish mother entrusted her child.

Miss Hoborough did not, of course, pour out all these details on the night of the birthday ball. Having listened to her sister's last message and effectively dried Marjie's tears by sending her off to brew fresh negus—the first bowl having cooled untasted —she was anxious to hear the rest of Charmian's story. Her interest prolonged a very simple recital to such lengths that the two older ladies were smothering their yawns with increasing frequency before it was done.

She stopped at last. "But I forget myself," she exclaimed apologetically. "It is quite shockingly late— or rather early," she amended, smiling. "You must all be utterly weary. Tomorrow—today—there will be time to gather up the lost years. And you will forgive me, my dear," she turned to Charmian, "for my doubts. I daresay you thought me harsh, unfeeling. But there are such things as impostors, you know, especially where there is a good deal at stake." And Charmian, growing drowsy, and longing only for the privacy of her own room, where she could forget about ancient griefs and long lost relatives and indulge herself to the full in the blissful recollection of what Rolf had said and how he had looked, answered gently that there was nothing to forgive and bade her new-found aunt good-night. Though why there should be so much ado about so simple a matter was more than she could fathom.

The older ladies, of course, had perfectly understood what Miss Hoborough had meant by that reference to 'a good deal at stake' though they were too well-bred to exchange so much as a speaking glance until they, too, had retired for the night. They then agreed that the hint was unmistakeable. Charmian was to benefit in some way from the vast Hoborough wealth. They were too sleepy to speculate for long over the precise form, agreeing that time would reveal it soon enough, but since they were both sincerely fond of the girl they congratulated themselves and each other on their share in effecting this happy issue. For now, with Hoborough blood and Hoborough gold, the child might look as high as she chose in the matrimonial stakes.

It might have been supposed that after the startling disclosure which had terminated the birthday ball the older ladies at least would have lain long in bed next day, but it so chanced that all of them were preoccupied with thoughts and plans that dispelled fatigue and brought them punctually to the breakfast table. Charmian was looking for the arrival of Rolf and Jasper who were to escort them back to Medhurst. No definite time had been agreed for this but she felt it would not be long delayed. And once back at Medhurst they could announce their betrothal. Even Charmian was sufficiently worldly wise to be aware that the path of true love would undoubtedly be smoothed by her sudden acquisition of a creditable pedigree. She sighed gratefully, and applied herself to her breakfast with good appetite.

The three older ladies were skirmishing cautiously around the arrangement of Charmian's future. Miss Hoborough rather naturally assumed that her niece would spend most of her days between Brent Abbas and Cheyne Walk, until such time as she married—an event which opened up a vast field of delightful speculation. She put forward the suggestion that Charmian should spend the next few weeks at Brent Abbas so that they might improve their acquaintance, but made no demur when the girl said shyly that she would like to remain at Medhurst, at least for the duration of Lady Cecilia's visit. Much to Charmian's relief, all three ladies found this a very proper attitude. For her part she could not help regretting that a visit to Brent Abbas must mean close daily association with Mr. Stanton Hoborough. That gentleman had lingered in the breakfast room long enough to express, in a few well-chosen phrases, his delight in the amazing news that his aunt had imparted to him, and had then gone off for his morning ride, exclaiming archly that the ladies would have a great deal of wondering and exclaiming to do and would manage better without him. Somehow it did not ring true.

It was a comfort to know her true parentage at last, but she had no desire at all to cry cousins with Mr. Hoborough.

Rolf and Jasper arrived at Medhurst just before noon and were persuaded to join the ladies in a light repast. The strange tale was unfolded by several eager speakers and received in characteristic fashion, Jasper making much mischievous by-play over addressing Charmian with exaggerated deference, Rolf listening more soberly. There was no opportunity, at Brent Abbas, for so much as one word in private, but he seized the first opportunity of drawing her aside once they were back at Medhurst.

She went with him very willingly. Now they could forget everything but themselves and their plans for the future. But his first words made her feel oddly uneasy. All the confident assurance of the previous evening was gone. He took her hand, to be sure, and smiled down at her, but the smile had a rueful twist as he said slowly, "I could wish that this revelation had occurred sooner—or not at all."

She was puzzled. "Do you not care for the Hoborough connection?" she asked timidly.

He shook his head. "Say rather that your new relations will think *me* far beneath *your* touch," he told her, and at the indignant protest in her face went on quietly. "Try to understand, love. You are no longer alone in the world nor even modestly circumstanced. Your whole situation has changed. You will be the cherished darling of one of Society's most influential hostesses. Very probably you are also an heiress. Your future is rich with promise. Your aunt cannot be expected to go into ecstasies over the prospect of your marriage to a poverty-stricken farmer. I make no doubt she is already weaving her plans for you."

"Then it is a sad waste of her time. And since I am of age, she must resign herself, for I'll marry my poverty-stricken farmer or no one."

At this declaration of loyalty he must bestow a grateful hug upon her, an action followed inevitably by kisses, convincingly enthusiastic. But this happy interlude was all too brief. Though he still held her close, there was quiet determination in his voice as he explained that to keep her to her promise, now, when her future was so bright and fair, would be to take advantage of her inexperience.

Against that gentle inflexibility, Charmian argued and protested in vain until presently she fell into thoughtful silence. Opposition, it seemed, would not serve. But she had no mind to let her precious newfound happiness escape so easily. She guessed that masculine pride had a good deal to do with this latest quirk. The gentleman would be happy to play Cophetua to the beggar maid but he did not care for it when the roles were reversed. Well—she liked him the better for that—and was still less inclined to risk losing him for some high-sounding notion of honourable conduct. She felt that something must be done to put matters on a proper footing before he went back to Ryelands. If once he withdrew to that safe fastness, goodness only knew what shifts she might be put to, and even *her* resolution shrank from the prospect of pursuing him into Suffolk. But perhaps that sensitive pride of his might be made to serve her purpose.

She withdrew herself gently but decisively from his arms and said steadily, "Very well. You wish to cry off?"

That struck home just as she had hoped it would. He said fiercely that it was no such thing; that if he followed only his own inclination, he would carry her off forthwith and marry her out of hand. It was only that she must be given the opportunity of meeting someone who might please her more—provide more adequately for her comfort and happiness.

Charmian wasted no time on this foolish suggestion. Had she not already had ample time to meet this non-existent paragon? Instead she pursued her advantage.

"What you really wish," she told him thoughtfully, "is that we should defer the announcement of our engagement for the time being."

It was not in the least what he had wished, but so hard on the heels of his latest avowal he could scarcely insist that they were *not* engaged—that he wished her to consider herself perfectly free.

"It would be a sensible solution," he admitted reluctantly.

"Yes. Very well indeed for the world at large. And I freely consent to it," that scheming young miss told him. "But"—demurely—"I do not quite like to deceive your Mama, who has been so kind to me. Do you not think that we might lay our difficulties before her? And be guided by her advice as to how long we should wait?"

Mama was probably the last person he would have chosen as confidante and counsellor. With her impractical and romantic disposition she would see no cause for this heart searching, would have the pair of them married in a pig's whisper and move on without a check to blissful anticipation of hordes of grandchildren. But he was out-generalled and knew it. He submitted meekly.

Lady Medhurst's views were much as he had expected. What could be more delightful than a marriage between her adored son and the girl who was already as dear to her as a daughter? But rather surprisingly she thought it a very good notion that the announcement should be a little delayed, though her reason was for other than her son's. She suggested that it would be unkind to snatch away Miss Hoborough's long-lost niece so soon. Rolf and Charmian were young. It would not hurt them to spare a little time to pleasure that frail, indomitable lady.

"But how long must we wait?" asked Charmian rather doubtfully.

"Oh—a month—perhaps two," said Lady Medhurst cheerfully. "You are already promised to spend some weeks at Brent Abbas. We shall see how matters go."

"And you will write to me?" Charmian turned to Rolf.

Almost he capitulated there and then, so appealing were the big dark eyes, the quiver in the soft voice.

"I will write to you," he promised, "and look greedily for your replies, though I will not promise you love letters in the high romantic style. You are more like to get a complaint about the low price of pigs, or the difficulties of getting sour land into good heart. Meanwhile you must enjoy the fleshpots of Brent Abbas while you may."

THIRTEEN

CHARMIAN HAD BEEN VERY DUBIOUS about those fleshpots. The actuality proved to be surprisingly pleasant. Miss Hoborough was a delightful hostess. Her niece was to regard Brent Abbas as her home and to do just as she chose, but there were always casual suggestions for her entertainment. Between leisurely exploration of the old house and its treasures, driving about the estate to be introduced to various tenants and pensioners who remembered her mother, and playing the part of daughter of the house at one or two select gatherings of her aunt's friends, the days passed swiftly enough.

She also found a horrid fascination in listening to her aunt's careless references to the way in which the Hoborough children had been brought up at Brent Abbas half a century ago. A rigid discipline, almost unbelievable by Charmian's modern notions, had been accepted without question. But small wonder that those children, growing in maturity, had all eventually rebelled. Aunt Tabitha's dabblings in revolutionary philosophy, her own mother's elopement, were perfectly understandable. Slowly she pieced together a picture of her grandfather as a man eaten up by his own self-righteousness, determined that his children should accept his bigoted religious beliefs and humbly submit to his plans for them. His only son had been christened Samuel and destined from birth for the Church. Miss Hoborough's references to her brother were infrequent and brief, but Charmian gathered that he had not fulfilled his father's plan. On this one topic her aunt was not expansive. She spoke with affection of Sammy as a little boy, but there were no reference to his later career.

As for Cousin Stanton—Samuel's son—he was behaving beautifully. He addressed her as Cousin, with a comic gravity that suggested he found the relationship both delightful and entertaining. He was always at hand to explain things that interested her. He persuaded her to ride with him each morning, choosing a gentle animal well suited to her inexperience and offering sound advice and judicious encouragement, and he was never too busy to attend the ladies on their strolling walks about the grounds, or to drive them himself if they wished to go further afield. Not once did he betray any emotion that went beyond the bounds of kinship and gradually she came to believe that he had accepted her refusal as final.

Her visit stretched into a third week and then a fourth. The days were full and interesting and had it not been for her longing for Rolf and her frustration over the delay in their marriage plans, Charmian would have been quite content. Towards the end of his furlough, Jasper came to make his adieux, travelling past from Ryelands where he had been spending a few days with Rolf. He was on his way to Medhurst, and since he must pass within a mile of Brent Abbas had thought that he might impose upon his revered Miss Hoborough's hospitality. A breather for the horses—a tankard of ale, perhaps, for himself? This with such a beguiling look that she chuckled despite herself, told him that he was an arrant rogue, and insisted that he stay to lunch.

It seemed that she had a penchant for arrant rogues of this particular stamp, for she monopolised his attention throughout the meal, subjecting him to a searching interrogation as to his career and prospects. He accepted this with perfect good humour, informing her, though with something of a twinkle, that army life in peace time was a dead bore and that he had serious thoughts of selling out and setting up as a country gentleman, like Cousin Rolf.

"My father would like it well enough," he added, rather more seriously. "Always had a fancy for farming, he says, and reckons it would suit him very well to come and meddle with my management, so he'd be quite happy to put up the dibs. But I don't know. How if Boney was to get loose again? I'd look silly then, wouldn't I?"

Miss Hoborough grunted, and enquired if he thought his Cousin Rolf a happy example of a country gentleman. "Shabby and purse-pinched, practically a recluse, and concerned only with the vagaries of the weather and the disastrous effects of the peace on farm prices."

"Well he seems happy enough at the moment," returned Jasper, with an amused sidelong glance at Charmian's indignant face, "though to be sure the place was in an uproar. He told me that as there was naught to be done in the fields in this weather he'd set the men to refurbishing the house and buildings. Better than throwing them out of work, I suppose, but small comfort for a guest. I lived in imminent dread of being invited to sweep a chimney or paint a ceiling."

"Can he be thinking of marrying?" demanded Miss Hoborough, deeply interested. "High time, if he is. But who? None of your war-time mushroom heiresses will do for a Heriot. Good blood will be his first thought, and money a long way second, though money is what he needs with Medhurst draining him of every penny."

She fell silent, so obviously deep in thought that the three younger folk respected her abstraction and conversed in low murmurs for several minutes until she suddenly emerged to announce, "Well—he *is* my godson. I had meant to remember him in my Will. But if he marries a girl I can approve, I shall make it a wedding gift. He is a sensible hard-working boy and I daresay the money will do him more good at this stage of his career. Which reminds me that I must see Hogan about changing my Will. If I were to write to him, perhaps you would take the letter to Town with you, Jasper. I shall want him to come down to Brent Abbas for a day or two. There is a good deal to be thought of."

Jasper being very willing to oblige her in this way she went off to write her letter, telling him that he might take Charmian to stroll through the conservatories for a while since she didn't suppose he had come a mile out of his way just for the pleasure of *her* society. Nephew Stanton looked a little put out at this suggestion but could scarcely intervene in face of so plain a directive.

Miss Hoborough's assumption was, in fact, perfectly accurate. Jasper had brought a letter from Rolf, which must be tucked away in Charmian's reticule to be savoured at leisure. He also brought word that Rolf would be visiting Medhurst the following week on business and might find time to ride over to Brent Abbas to see how she did. And if he was not actually informed of the understanding between Charmian and his cousin, it was plain that he had a pretty shrewd idea of the way matters stood. He teased her a little for having put the sober, practical Rolf in such a taking and wanted to know if the two of them really meant to make a match of it, but he did not press for answers when he saw her confusion. Instead he told her more about the work that was in progress at Ryelands. By his light-hearted account the place was being turned into a positive palace. Charmian listened, and laughed at his droll descriptions, her heart warm with happiness at the thought of all the care and effort that was being expended on her insignificant self, and went back to the house in such a glow of delight that even Miss Hoborough sensed the lift in her spirits, while Stanton's eyes narrowed and his brows drew together in an expression that boded ill for someone.

The rest of the week passed smoothly. Charmian's precious letter—which mentioned neither the price of pigs nor any other agricultural topic—grew limp and crumpled from much reading. Stanton seemed to be unusually quiet and withdrawn. Miss Hoborough talked a good deal about Jasper, but her leading questions evoked no response from a sublimely unconscious Charmian, and eventually, having delivered herself of the opinion that military men, however charming, did *not* make satisfactory husbands, she abandoned the unprofitable pursuit. Her nephew, who had accorded her remarks a good deal more attention and understanding than they had received from her niece, smiled faintly, and returned to his task of checking some accounts connected with repairs to one of the farms. Since Miss Hoborough's sight had failed, he had taken over many such routine tasks.

He was not, however, invited to attend her conference with her attorney. She was in an irascible mood that morning. She brusquely informed her two young relatives that there was no need for them to be hanging about the house all day, and though the skies were still threatening, practically drove them out of doors.

"She is always in a twitty mood when she is obliged to think about her Will," apologised Stanton gravely. "I suppose it *is* a gloomy business, evoking, as it must, thoughts of one's own mortality. Pray do not heed it. Would you like a stroll down to the lake, or should we be wiser to stay near the house in case of more rain? Then we could take shelter in the conservatories if necessary."

Charmian having elected to take the risk of a wetting, he waited only until they had put some little distance between themselves and the house before continuing. "For my own part, I am glad of this opportunity to be private with you. I have long wished to advert to a topic very near to my heart, but have waited as patiently as I might in the hope that the closer acquaintance that we have enjoyed during these past weeks might dispose you to listen to me more sympathetically. Do you not agree that we have gone on very comfortably together? It is my earnest hope that you will now reconsider your first refusal of my plea, and will consent to bestow your hand upon me. I have shown you, I trust, that I can be both patient and indulgent—qualities very desirable in a husband. But although I have not teased you with repeated importunities, I would not have you doubt my ardour. Come now! Will you not relent, and make me happy?"

Poor Charmian! Even in her dismay she could not help contrasting this prosaic and slightly pompous speech with Rolf's methods. This was a very tepid lover! But even though his passion was of a temperate kind he doubtless had feelings that could be hurt like any other man. Frantically she sought for some phrases in which to reject him, quite finally, but without inflicting unnecessary humiliation, and it seemed to her that the truth—or part of it—would serve best.

"I believed that you had accepted my decision as final, Cousin," she said quietly. "Had I dreamed that you nourished hopes of persuading me to change my mind, I would have told you that my promise is already given to another. If this knowledge distresses you I am truly sorry, but I have never regarded you as other than a friend and, latterly, a cousin. I can only repeat that there must be a number of delightful girls, beautiful and well-born, any one of whom would make you a far more suitable wife than ever I could be."

For just one moment his air of well-bred serenity was shattered. Some emotion—savage—inimical—

blazed in the fine eyes. Disappointment? Jealousy? Wounded pride? It was subdued almost immediately, though not before he had said bitterly, "The glamour of a scarlet coat has a good deal to answer for. I had credited you with more good sense. But so be it. Your fate is on your own head."

As the valediction of a rejected lover it lacked something of grace and generosity but at least it allayed any pangs of guilt that Charmian might have suffered. She suppressed the impulse to inform him that scarlet coats had nothing to say in the matter. Her marriage plans were none of his business. If he chose to think her in love with Jasper it was quite his own fault—and Jasper would think it a great joke. She was grateful when a sudden flurry of rain drove them back to shelter, and spent the rest of the forenoon in her own room, perturbed and shaken by the unpleasant ending to her morning stroll, reading her precious letter yet again for reassurance.

She went down to luncheon in some apprehension but only her aunt and Mr. Hogan put in an appearance and she was soon pleasantly distracted by the lawyer's interest in her strange history. By the time that she and Stanton met again at dinner her cousin had recovered his usual poise. Perhaps he realised that he had not appeared to advantage in the morning's encounter. Certainly he was at some pains to be pleasant, entering with interest into his aunt's plans for the parties that she proposed to give when they returned to Town. Charmian felt very uncomfortable. All of these hopeful schemes assumed her continued presence as a member of the household, and common civility obliged her to join in the discussion though she felt that her tacit acceptance was sheer deceit. When her aunt proceeded to a thoughtful, if slightly acid, enumeration of the eligible gentlemen who were to be invited to these distinguished gatherings, she was sure that there was a malicious gleam behind her cousin's expression of courteous attention. She remembered thankfully that she had promised to perform some charitable errands for her aunt on the following day. Short of downright rudeness she could scarcely avoid the morning ride, but equestrian exercise gave little opportunity for intimate conversation and she could quite legitimately excuse herself from any further excursions in his company.

It seemed, however, that she need not put herself to such pains. At breakfast he told her, with apparent regret, that this morning's ride would be the last for a sennight at least. Business matters demanded his return to Town.

His attitude during the ride had reverted to the easy, cousinly one that she preferred. Only as they were returning to the house did he turn briefly to more personal matters, breaking in upon her stilted farewell utterances—trusting that his business affairs would prosper and that they might look for his early return.

"No need for the flummery, cousin," he said, a hint of a smile softening the rough words. "I'm well aware that I behaved badly yesterday and that you will be thankful to see the back of me. Set it to my credit that my business on Town is none so urgent that it could not have waited." And strode off to his own quarters without giving her a chance to reply.

The blunt utterance certainly softened her feelings towards him, though he had spoken no more than truth and she would breathe more easily when he was gone. She hastened to change her riding dress for a plain morning gown and went down to the housekeeper's room where three well-filled baskets were ready for her.

"They're heavy, miss," warned Mrs. Morton. "Will you have the gig ordered round?"

Charmian weighed them in her hand. "Whose is this? Mrs. Ventry's?"

Mrs. Morton nodded.

"Then I'll walk across the park with it this morning. The other two can wait till after lunch. Will you tell Thomas I shall want the gig this afternoon?"

She set off briskly. The errand would take the better part of an hour, and that was not allowing for the time that she must spend in listening to the old woman's rambling tales of a life spent in Hoborough service. With a little luck her cousin would have left for Town before she returned.

But her luck was out. She had decided to cross

the park by a grassy ride which made pleasanter walking than the main drive, but she had scarcely turned into it when she heard her name spoken. Stanton was approaching her from the direction of the stables, and as he came up he said with a rueful smile, "It seems my adieux were a little premature. I had hoped to be on the road by now but Titus had a shoe loose. Tenby has taken him to the smith's. May I walk with you a little way, cousin? It will be half an hour at least before he is back. And if you would care for it, I could show you something of the Abbey ruins. It is not wise to walk there alone, for they are sadly decayed. Much that was standing when I was a lad is already fallen."

She was not particularly enamoured of the idea but it was difficult to refuse, though she *did* wish that he would offer to carry the basket, which seemed to grow heavier with every step. Either Rolf or Jasper would have performed the simple service without a second thought, but Cousin Stanton evidently felt that he was doing more than enough by entertaining her with tales of boyhood exploits in the ancient precincts, and did not even notice that she had difficulty in keeping up with his long steps.

She was thankful for a chance to catch her breath while he pointed out the remains of the nave and cloisters and showed her where the refectory and hospice had stood. She found it all rather depressing. The patient, loving labour of so many hands— and all brought to ruin by a changing social system and the ravages of time and weather, though here and there were glimpses of its former dignity and beauty—a trefoiled window—a delicately moulded arch, framing a lovely vista of woodland.

"But this is the most interesting bit," announced her guide, leading the way down a walk that was in a slightly better state of preservation. "I discovered it quite by accident and I have never shown it to anyone else. So you see you are greatly honoured, cousin!"

It was an honour that Charmian could well have dispensed with. The massive walls seemed to be closing in on her. They shut out the sunlight, and the place smelled of damp and mildew. The flagged floor was treacherous and slimy. She was on the edge of protest when her cousin stopped.

"Here we are. It's a bit dark, but I think I can manage. I was used to bringing a candle lantern, and I daresay it is still here. We shall soon see."

He put both hands to a stone that projected from one wall and pushed it with some force. There was a harsh grating noise and a section of the wall pivoted, barring further progress but leaving an aperture that loomed inky black in the dim light. Charmian shivered. The place was about as inviting as an open tomb, but her cousin appeared to think that he was giving her a high treat.

"Wait just a moment until I see if the steps are still safe," he admonished. "Can't have you turning an ankle," and vanished from her side. She heard his receding footsteps, and, presently, an exclamation of satisfaction.

"It's still here!" he called back to her, his voice booming oddly from the black depths below. "Stay where you are till I kindle a light."

She was very willing to obey. And the wavering glow that presently rewarded his efforts only seemed to make the surrounding darkness thicker. She had certainly no intention of risking the descent by *that* feeble illumination.

"Can't you see?" he called up to her, a hint of impatience in his tone. And then, before she could answer, "Not scared of the dark, are you?"

She thought there was amusement and satisfaction in his voice, and wondered briefly if he had brought her here deliberately, to torment and to frighten— to punish her for a rejection that had hurt his self-consequence; but his reply to her indignant denial was pleasant enough, as he bade her wait until he brought the light nearer. He took her arm to steady her, holding the lantern aloft with his free hand so that she could watch her footing.

There was little enough to see, even when the descent was finally accomplished and her eyes had grown accustomed to the darkness; a low stone slab set against one wall that might have been used as bench or table, a stone grille in another. This might have been designed to admit air and light but was now thickly overgrown with ivy. Charmian could see nothing to appeal, even to an adventurous small boy. She said politely, "What do you suppose it was used for? A safe hiding place for the abbey's treasures?"

He shrugged. "Perhaps. More likely a punishment cell. There is no way of opening the door from within. A man would have ample time for repentance, immured here, and none to hear his anguished pleas."

Charmian shrank. "Horrid! I cannot imagine how you ever dared to venture in here alone and shall be heartily thankful to return to daylight and sweeter air."

"Yes," he agreed gently. "A pity that I find myself obliged to deny you that very understandable desire. But it is quite your own fault, you know. If only you had consented to marry me, I should not have been put to such a distasteful necessity. You left me no choice."

Before she could fully grasp the import of his words he had darted swiftly up the crumbling stairway. In stunned disbelief she stared at the figure outlined in the opening at the top. Then, as she realised that he had spoken in deadly earnest, she sprang desperately forward, stumbled over an uneven flagstone, and fell on hands and knees at the foot of the steps.

From above her came the light, drawling voice. "Do not put yourself to the pains of climbing, cousin. Though in general I would shrink from the thought of offering physical violence to a female,

I should certainly steel myself to thrust you down again. And then, you know, you might be called upon to suffer all the pain of a broken limb, in addition to the pangs of hunger and thirst which, I fear, I cannot spare you."

"But you *cannot* mean to leave me here to die of starvation."

"No? You stand between me and a fortune, my dear. A fortune that has kept me all my days dancing attendance on a cantankerous old woman. Why should I resign any part of it to you? I grant that I had rather our dear aunt stood in your place, since I believe that she has not yet signed her new Will. But it would not do, you know. Where *you* are concerned it will readily be believed that you wandered in here out of idle curiosity—if you are ever found, of course. My aunt's presence would certainly arouse undesirable speculation. You see the difficulty? It is sad that one so young and fair should perish so miserably, but as I pointed out, it is quite your own fault. You were perfectly comfortably established in Wivelsfield. So long as you remained there you posed no threat to my inheritance. I have known of your existence, you see, these ten years and more— ever since I was sent to Brittany to hunt for you. But first you must needs thrust yourself into Society —when it became only a matter of time before someone recognised you—and then, when I had brought myself to accept the distasteful necessity of marrying you, you must needs prefer that puppy in a scarlet coat. Well—you might have married your Jasper with my very good will, but you shall not rob Stanton Hoborough of his hard-earned inheritance."

The flood of his eloquence washed over her, leaving her only half comprehending, but one thing at least was abundantly clear. It would be of no avail to beg for mercy. The light, callous voice was quite pitiless, and even in her extremity she would not give him the satisfaction of listening to her broken pleas. She wondered vaguely if that was what he was waiting for.

He said abruptly, "By the way—it is of no use to wear out your pretty voice in calling for help. In the unlikely event of anyone hearing your cries, they would serve only to strengthen the local belief that the Abbey is haunted. And now, I regret that I must leave you. I plan to reach Town before you are missed. You may keep the light to frighten the ghosts away—and to permit you to test the security of your—er—accommodation. For the last time, cousin, I bid you adieu."

FOURTEEN

THE ROUGH SQUEAL OF THE CLOSING door seemed to echo endlessly in her ears. A great wave of terror and despair engulfed her as she still crouched at the foot of the stairway. Above, the candle lantern glimmered faintly, and her first coherent thought, as the daze of sudden disaster began to recede, was that there were but three or four inches of candle remaining. Soon total darkness would complete her misery. But since she had no means of kindling a light, there was no point in saving those precious remaining inches for a time of greater need.

She rose, stiffly—the chill of the place already seeping into her limbs—and began to climb the steps, aimlessly, yet drawn by the light. She had no plan, no hope, but the candle flame was the only suggestion of life in the hideous tomb. She even spread out her hands to catch the illusion of warmth —and as she did so her sleeve brushed against the basket that she had set down before essaying the descent. Even then, for a moment, she did not fully comprehend the importance of that basket. Not until her fingers touched the woollen shawl that was tucked over its contents did she remember that the basket contained food. What kind of food she did not know, but the candle would last long enough to show her.

With trembling care she carried first the basket and then the lantern to the stone slab, wrapped the shawl about her shoulders, and proceeded to investigate.

Miss Hoborough had been generous. There were eggs and beef jelly, some slices of chicken and a large sponge cake, a bottle of port wine, from which the cork had been drawn and carefully replaced, and a fine bunch of grapes. Not being practically toothless, as was the proper recipient, Charmian could have wished for something more substantial, but one does not disparage the gifts of the Gods. Besides, the basket represented more than food. Cousin Stanton might have set his trap very cleverly, and she been fool enough to fall into it, but he had made at least two mistakes. It was beneath his dignity to carry a basket—and that had left her with the means to survive for a good deal longer than he must have anticipated. And he did not know about Rolf. Rolf, who could certainly be trusted to take the Abbey ruins apart stone by stone when he found that she was missing. Hope rose within her. A man who could make two vital mistakes might have made more. He might even have been seen near the ruins, or have left some careless clue that would help the searchers. She would certainly ignore his advice about calling for help.

The candle flared up, reminding her that its life was nearly done. Hastily, but carefully, she set out the provisions on the bench, leaving the eggs in the basket lest they should roll and break, placing the other viands where she could easily identify them by touch, and telling herself firmly that she was not in the least hungry. Thirst would probably be the greatest hardship, though the grapes would help a little. Thirst, and cold. She wrapped the shawl more closely about her arms and shoulders and began to walk up and down the cell. Somehow she must try to keep life and warmth in herself until help arrived.

The candle flickered, dwindled and died.

Mr. Hoborough had, in fact, been seen in the vicinity of the ruins. But since no one associated this fact with Charmian's disappearance the place was searched in rather perfunctory fashion since it was considered unlikely to yield results. She had not been really missed until evening, her empty place at lunch causing Miss Hoborough to decide that she had stayed over-long with Mrs. Ventry, but when she had not returned by dinner time it was realised that something was amiss. Enquiry of Mrs. Ventry eliciting the fact that she had not so much as set eyes on young miss, a search of the grounds was instituted, and it was not until this proved fruitless that any serious alarm was felt. For what harm could befall a young lady in the peaceful English countryside? It was not even as though she had been riding or driving, when one might have been obliged to consider the possibility of serious accident.

But by this time darkness prevented effective search. Waiting through the long hours of the night, dropping occasionally into a brief uneasy doze, waking to the recital of repeated failure as the search parties straggled back to report, Miss Hoborough had reached the limit of her strength by daylight. For perhaps the first time in her strong-minded existence she craved support and comfort. A groom was despatched to Town to bid her nephew return immediately, and for herself she ordered the carriage brought round to convey her to Medhurst. Philip Heriot was one of her oldest friends. Even in his invalid state he could bring a masculine mind to bear on her troubles, while the thought of Mary's concern and sympathy was infinitely comforting.

Her unexpected arrival caused some surprise. Lady Medhurst came hurrying in, all agog to discover what had brought her, but at the sight of the wan, anxious face, curiosity turned to shocked dismay. She caught Miss Hoborough's cold shaking hands in her own firm clasp and guided her to a chair by the fire, directing Noakes to bring wine and cakes while she herself removed the guest's bonnet, murmuring the while the kind of soothing noises that she might have bestowed upon a frightened child.

Under the effect of this treatment, the haughty, icily-composed Miss Hoborough burst into harsh, desperate sobs and had to be patted and soothed back to coherence before her hostess could make any sense out of the farrago of broken utterances that emerged from her lips. But as the wine exerted its restorative effect and the story began to take shape in all its puzzling simplicity, Lady Medhurst's horror and distress fully equalled the narrator's. She stared at her with dilated eyes, and could only murmur feebly, "But she can't just have vanished!"

Miss Hoborough stared back, numb and hopeless. There was a painful silence.

"Abduction?" faltered Lady Medhurst presently. "For ransom? Because she is *your* niece."

That brought a faint flicker of hope. "If that is so it shall be paid whatever the demand," pronounced Miss Hoborough, with something of her old determination. "But until some demand is sent to us, we can do nothing."

They debated the desirability of admitting Lord Medhurst into their counsels, Miss Hoborough, calmer now that she had shared the burden of responsibility, reluctant to unfold so tragic a tale to one in poor health, but both ladies feeling strongly that the case called for that powerful grasp of essential facts, those prompt decisions and swift actions in which the male sex were undoubtedly superior.

The discussion was cut short by sounds of arrival. Lady Medhurst, who had temporarily forgotten her son's impending visit, gave a little cry of thankfulness that he should appear just when he was so sorely needed, and flung herself into his outstretched arms, pouring out the tale of disaster in swift breathless phrases. Rolf's face grew grim as he listened, interrupting once or twice to question Miss Hoborough. A whole day she had been missing, his little love, and no one with the least idea as to what could have befallen her. Instinct urged him to set out for Brent Abbas to seek her for himself, but good sense insisted that it could not be so simple. The search must indeed be continued, its field extended; and those areas that had been covered in bad light would have to be gone over again. Time was becoming vitally important, but better to spend a little of it now, in careful planning. And on one point at least he had no doubts. His father must certainly be apprised of the whole.

"If only because we were to have discussed business this morning, and he will naturally wonder why I cannot do so, but also because his knowledge of the neighbourhood will be useful, while any fresh mind brought to bear on the mystery may produce just the clue that we need. Nor do I think you need fear for his fortitude. He has been so much better of late, his mind quite clear. I think you will find him well able to advise and support us in this crisis, as she would certainly wish to do."

So indeed it proved. Lord Medhurst listened to their story with grave concern and appeared to grasp the facts of the case without difficulty. His own experience prompted him to suggest loss of memory as a possible explanation for Charmian's disappearance. Quite a minor accident could have caused it, and in such a case the victim might have wandered some distance. He did not wholly reject the abduction theory, but thought it improbable.

"Scarcely anyone knows as yet that Charmian *is* your niece," he pointed out, "and there would be small profit to be got from abducting an unknown girl."

Both ladies derived some comfort from his calm and practical manner. A suggestion that his wife should return to Brent Abbas with Miss Hoborough to support her through the ordeal of waiting for news, was also well received. It was not until he was left alone with his son, Lady Medhurst having gone off to her own room to make the necessary preparations, bearing her friend with her, that he said soberly, "But if you do not find her by the darkening we shall have to consider the possibility of crime. That means Bow Street."

"And a resounding clamour which we shall none of us enjoy. But I am not prepared to wait until tonight. With your permission, Papa, I'll send one of your grooms to Bow Street at once, with a letter detailing the circumstances. Better to raise the alarm prematurely than waste further precious time. Then I'll be off to Brent Abbas."

Unfortunately the representative of Bow Street who arrived in answer to this urgent summons was ill at ease in a rural setting. Bereft of his customary sources of information, of the list of habitual criminals who sprang readily to mind when it was a case of a Town house burgled or a wealthy citizen waylaid and robbed, he seemed singularly inept to the deeply anxious Rolf. And several of his solemn routine questions were unfortunately delivered within Miss Hoborough's hearing, putting her in a fine taking.

"And 'oo," he enquired portentously, "stands to benefit if the young lady dies untimely?"

The question did nothing to calm Miss Hoborough's nervous fears. It *did* give her seriously to think; the more so when a weary groom returned from a fruitless errand. Mr. Hoborough was gone out of Town, he reported. No one knew where, though one stable boy had a vague notion that he might ha' nipped across to Ireland, where a zealous bailiff bred hacks and hunters on Hoborough land. Why should Stanton have gone off just at this juncture? He had never done so before, was always meticulous about leaving his direction with her in case she should need him. But he *could* not have had anything to do with—Hastily she dismissed the monstrous thought as a nightmare, induced by lack of sleep and crushing anxiety.

Throughout the day and long after dusk the search went on, the weary seekers reinforced now by volunteers from neighbouring villages who, in the immemorial way of country folk, had 'chanced to hear' the shocking news. But their efforts went unrewarded. The gentleman from Bow Street had early abandoned the local search, transferring his attention to the posting inns, the points at which a stage might be boarded, and any other hostelry where transport could be hired, but his painstaking enquiries proved equally fruitless.

"Nary 'ide nor 'air of 'er," he reported, scratching his nose in puzzled fashion. "Less it's an elopement —which I takes it you've no call to suspicion that— I'd say she's never left the place. Must be some place you've never thought to look. Could she 'ave got locked in somewhere by haccident? Rooms aplenty in this great rambling place—and old enough for locks to jam."

Wearily dismissing this naive suggestion, Rolf outlined his plans for the night. In half an hour the moon would be up and the search could continue. Meanwhile food had been prepared by such of the staff as were too old to join in the search, and was set out in the kitchen. He advised his lieutenant to take advantage of this provision with all speed.

For himself he could not endure the company of his fellows or their kind-hearted attempts at comfort. Not the least part of his agony was his knowledge of personal responsibility. If only he had yielded to Charmian's wishes—not insisted on this Brent Abbas visit and a delay in their marriage plans—why—they might even have been married by now, and she safe in his keeping at Ryelands. He drove a clenched fist savagely into the padded window seat on which he had flung himself down. All for the sake of pride—stubborn, stiffnecked fool that he was—and perhaps he had sent his darling to her death.

A lightening in the night sky roused him from his agony of helplessness. The moon was rising—and thank God for a fine clear night. There was some relief to be found in action. He drained the tankard of ale that had stood neglected at his elbow and bit absent-mindedly into a substantial sandwich. He did not taste it. But he had eaten nothing since his early breakfast and stood in need of sustenance.

The sound of wheels on the gravel brought him to his feet. News? More likely another party of neighbours come to offer help, he decided, and took a second sandwich just as a flustered maid tapped at the door and announced, "Lord Medhurst, sir."

For a man who had not set foot outside his own gates for the better part of a year, his lordship looked remarkably at ease. True, he leaned rather heavily on his stick, while the watchful Butterbeck hovered attentively at his other side, but his breathing was even, his colour good, and he brushed Butterbeck aside quite impatiently when that devoted soul, having installed him in a high-backed chair, tried to provide him with a foot-stool.

"Stop fussing, man. I'm done with being wrapped in cotton. The drive and the air have done me more good than months of coddling. But you can go and bring me some of those sandwiches," he added more kindly, "and something to drink. Ale will do." He nodded the man imperatively to the door and turned to his startled son.

"Couldn't endure the waiting," he said briefly. "Wanted to be here, at the heart of things. Besides, I took a notion. Didn't want Butterbeck listening though. Might be all a hum. Take it you've no news?"

Rolf shook his head and awaited further enlightenment, but his father seemed oddly reluctant to proceed. His air of brisk satisfaction in returning vigour was gone, and a heavy frown had taken its place. Presently he fetched an uncomfortable sigh and said abruptly, "Don't like to speak ill of a fellow without proof, but needs must. Never did care for young Hoborough above half. An oily customer— and hanging on his aunt's sleeve—no way for a man to go on. Bad blood, too. Less said about his mother, the better. And Sam Hoborough was a reckless good-for-naught, with a fatal weakness for bad company. His sister would tell you 'twasn't his fault. Kept on too tight a rein in his youth. But I doubt if even she knew the full tale of his misdeeds and—yes—crimes. Every kind of excess and debauchery. Beggar's Club—witchcraft—the Black Mass—'twas said *that* was the only use he ever made of his training for the Church. High priest of their coven, he was, and the wench he married tainted with the same vile perversions. No knowing when the same evil streak might show up in the son. That's what I'm afraid of. It's an odd coincidence that he should have gone off too. Could *he* have abducted the girl? With a view to forcing her into marriage. Your mother believes that he *did* ask for her, and was refused. He's not one to take kindly to refusal. Though I daresay it was the money that prompted the offer in the first instance."

"Money?" interjected Rolf, somewhat overwhelmed by this flow of revelation from his normally taciturn parent.

"Stands to lose a handsome sum by the child's survival," grunted his father. "You can lay to it that Tabitha will do the right thing. Her sister's share of the Hoborough money will go to Charmian."

Rolf nodded thoughtfully. Money seemed unimportant in view of the present crisis, and surely no man would go to such shifts to secure it. Only filial respect obliged him to acknowledge the possibility. "I will certainly enquire more closely into the circumstances of his departure," he promised, "but I cannot abandon the search at this juncture. That fellow from Bow Street—Tipping—can look into it. Come to think of it, he *did ask* who stood to benefit if—if——" He broke off, refusing to put his growing dread into words.

"Send him in to me when you go," his father suggested. "We'll set about it between us. It will have to be discreetly handled. Don't want it coming to Tabitha's ears."

"She's laid upon her bed with Mama and old Marjie in attendance, so you're safe enough," returned his son, and went off to find the Runner.

There were the usual exasperating delays in eliciting the required information. The ancient coachman said that Mr. Stanton had taken his tilbury, and was garrulous about the mysteriously loosened shoe which had delayed his departure, with a good deal of self-exculpatory detail. But the groom who had taken the horse to the smithy was out with one of the search parties, and when these returned he was found to have lingered behind to visit his ailing mother. However, when he finally presented himself to a fuming Lord Medhurst, his recollection was clear enough.

He had brought the animal back from the smithy just on noon. Mr. Hoborough was not in the stables at that time. He himself had permission to go and see to his mother's dinner, she being bedfast, and on his way home he had crossed the green ride that led past the Abbey ruins towards the village and caught a glimpse of Mr. Hoborough approaching in the distance. He supposed him to have strolled along the ride by way of putting on the time.

"You had no speech with him, then?"

The groom coloured guiltily. "No, milord." And then, frankly, "I was late already, and I thought he'd keep me, complaining about Titus. I nipped across the ride smartish like, and don't think he saw me. Anyway he didn't call out."

"And you saw nothing of Miss Charmian?"

"No, milord."

"An honest lad," approved Mr. Tipping, when the groom had gone. "His tale agrees pretty well with what the 'ousekeeper told us. The young lady would 'ave been well down the ride before the lad crossed it. Didn't seem over-fond of the young gentleman, did 'e?"

Lord Medhurst did not answer directly. He said slowly, "He left here quite openly, driving a tilbury. No passenger. And reached Town at an hour that did not permit of any dawdling by the way. He could scarcely have had time to pick her up and to dispose of her, nor is a tilbury suited to such a purpose. It seems reasonably certain that he did *not* take her with him. So she is still here, and the business takes a more sinister turn."

"I'll not say but what yer could be right, guv'nor," allowed the Runner grudgingly. "But if she's 'ere, where is she? There's a few more byres and barns to search, but then we comes to an 'alt. And most places 'as been gone over a two-three times already.

No young lady could 'ave wandered further, and if she's a prisoner, where's 'e 'id 'er?"

Lord Medhurst linked his fingers beneath his chin and rested his elbows on the table as he considered the problem. Mentally he reviewed the Brent Abbas estate, following the direction of the grass ride as it threaded its way through wood and pasture to the village.

"The old Abbey," he said reflectively. "She would pass quite close to it."

"Aye, milord, so she would. But no sensible wench 'ud go poking about among a lot o' crumbling walls, specially when she was going on a herrand 'o mercy. What should take her there?"

"Perhaps Mr. Hoborough did," suggested his lordship drily.

Mr. Tipping looked dubious. "Happen so," he agreed politely. "But if 'e did, what for? There's not four walls left standing, and no roof to speak of. You couldn't 'ide a body there."

Lord Medhurst flinched slightly, mistaking the use of the final substantive.

"*Any*body, I meant, milord," corrected the Runner apologetically. "Couldn't 'ide so much as a new-born kitten. 'Cept for one or two dark passages the place is open to the sky."

"The anchorite's cell!" exclaimed Lord Medhurst suddenly. "It was sound enough when Sam Hoborough showed me the trick of it—but that's a long time ago."

Mr. Tipping looked puzzled. "What would that be, milord?"

"It was a cell occupied by a monk who had withdrawn entirely from the world," explained Lord Medhurst. "Once enclosed, he never left it. This one was built against the wall of the church, and there was an aperture through which the occupant could see the altar when Mass was said. And if memory serves me rightly, it was impossible to open the door from the inside. If you wished to hide something—or to prison someone securely—there could be no safer hold."

His ally was not fully convinced. In fact his professional reputation was at stake, since he, personally, had searched the ruins, the local helpers being reluctant to go near the place and muttering between themselves about haunts and evil spirits. Mr. Tipping had told them in a very superior way that he took no account of such things, nor had he seen or heard anything to substantiate their case. But neither, he assured Lord Medhurst, had he seen any place where one could secure a prisoner.

"You wouldn't," agreed his lordship calmly. "Not unless you took careful measurements, which naturally no one would think to do. Nevertheless I promise you that the cell existed in my boyhood, and if it still does, I think I can show you the knack of getting into it."

Since Lord Medhurst's enthusiasm seemed likely to outrun the resources of his still convalescent body, it was fortunate that a grim and weary Rolf returned from yet another fruitless search before his father had dragooned Mr. Tipping into setting out forthwith.

As the story was laid before him, a glimmer of hope dawned in the sombre eyes. Even so faint and fantastic a possibility was better than nothing. They would take the carriage. Yes, of course Papa must come, since only he knew exactly where to look, but equally certainly he must not attempt to ride. In any case, they would need the carriage if, by some miraculous chance, their quest was successful. Somehow he controlled his own urgent longing to set out at once; dealt patiently with the garden boy in his willing but clumsy attempts to harness an over-lively pair to the light travelling chaise, ensured an ample supply of candles and lanterns and saw to it that his father was well muffled against the midnight chill. But at last they were off, at a pace that caused Mr. Tipping to clutch anxiously at the edge of his seat.

Lord Medhurst's memory proved to be fully equal to the task he had set himself. Hesitating only once or twice he led his companions to the concealed doorway and indicated the stone on which it pivoted, though his own strength did not suffice to open it. His son made short work of this final obstacle and three lanterns were lifted high in anxious hope. Mr. Tipping was blessing himself and declaring that he never saw the like, but Rolf's quick ears had caught a low whimpering noise from the gloomy depths of the cell. He took the treacherous steps in a couple of leaps, the lantern light wavering wildly, to gather up the pitiful little creature that crouched beside the stone bench and cradle her close, while he murmured broken endearments and snatches of thankful prayer into the tangled curls.

She was in a pitiable state. Despite her best efforts she had gradually succumbed to the numbing cold and the horror of solitude and darkness. Her voice was worn to a husky croak from her repeated calls for help, her hands torn and bleeding from her efforts to tear the encroaching ivy from the grille. Worst of all, she did not seem to know them, and struggled frantically in Rolf's hold, her dazed eyes staring fearfully up at him, a desperate demented creature. But her small strength was soon spent. Her head fell back, the heavy lids closed over the fear-crazed eyes, and Rolf's joy and thankfulness were temporarily swamped by a surge of murderous fury for the blackguard whose callous greed had so reduced his darling.

The lust to kill glared from his eyes and roughened his voice as he said savagely, "Let's get out of this hell-hole before she recovers consciousness. If only I could lay hands on that smooth-spoken——" He choked. Lighted by the solicitous Mr. Tipping he carried his pathetic burden to the waiting carriage.

FIFTEEN

LATE AS IT WAS, ROLF SET OUT AT ONCE for Medhurst to bring Susan. In Charmian's present state he could not reach her, to comfort or reassure. Perhaps Susan could. Perhaps the links of trust and affection forged from childhood on, would help to draw the girl away from the borderland of horror in which she still seemed to be wandering, back to sanity and the joy of living. And it seemed that love had given him understanding, for his mother was able to tell him that the tormented little creature had yielded instinctively to Susan's competent handling and had fallen at last into a natural sleep.

For two days Susan alternately babied and bullied her, and Mary Medhurst, who took over the nursing while Susan slept, reported encouraging progress. Perhaps the effects of her dreadful experience would never be wholly healed. She would not have the door closed unless one of them sat beside her, and candles must be kept burning all night, but in other respects she was well on the way to recovery. The doctor had said that she might get up for a little while next day, and then Rolf should see for himself.

Once satisfied that her niece was found and likely to recover, Miss Hoborough had shut herself up in her own apartments with only Marjie in attendance. On the following day she issued one order. Every trace of the old Abbey was to be removed; the stone carted away and tipped into a disused quarry, the ground levelled and sown to pasture. Woodland trees could be planted later. Nothing was to be left to remind Charmian of her ordeal, or to bring danger to others.

After that there was silence. Her friends guessed that she was trying to come to terms with the proof of her nephew's villainy, and to decide what must be done about it. They saluted her courage, and left her undisturbed.

By the third day, Lord Medhurst, apparently much invigorated by his recent activities, announced that he could not be lingering on for ever at Brent Abbas. Mary could stay—*she* was making herself useful—and Rolf must await Miss Hoborough's decision as to what must be done in the matter of her nephew.

"You're practically one of the family, m'boy, so she can safely entrust that business to you. In any case, you'll be wanting to stay until you see that poor child in better case."

"I have no intention of leaving without her, said his son simply. "I should never have another peaceful moment. I mean to coax her into marrying me as soon as I procure a licence. Peace and security are what she needs, and once she is my wife I shall know how to ensure that she has them."

Lord Medhurst nodded sympathetically, and undertook to make enquiries about the licence. "Sanbury can see to it," he suggested. "A quiet ceremony, with no fuss, and carry your bride off to Ryelands. You'll be quiet enough there, and she can try her hand at rearing chickens or ducklings or some such. That will give her thoughts a new direction. No need to tell you to cosset her for a while."

Rolf actually smiled. "Scarcely poultry, at this season, Papa," he protested mildly. "But I take your point. Luckily one of the farm dogs is in whelp. I daresay the pups will supply just the kind of occupation that you had in mind. As for cossetting . . ." he smiled again. A smile of such gentle sweetness that his father nodded, well satisfied.

"Yes," he said reflectively, "let her be an eager, healthy child again, before she is a wife." And then, horrified at his own lapse into sentiment, went on briskly, "One good thing, at least, comes out of all this."

Rolf lifted an enquiring eyebrow.

"Tabitha will want this nasty business hushed up, you can lay your life on it. Well—daresay you would yourself, so long as all is made safe for the future. If the tale was to leak out, it would only delight the gossips, and do no good to any of us. And if she were to bring the girl out in style, the more likely it would be to leak out—especially with Master Stanton conspicuously absent. No. She'll probably be thankful enough to agree to a quiet wedding. After all, it's a creditable match, though I say it myself, and the girl comfortably established. What more could she want?"

"Some prospect of happiness for her, poor child," said Miss Hoborough quietly. She had come into the room unperceived, her bearing perhaps a little less erect and arrogant than of yore, but her manner perfectly composed. "And I understand that I must look to you"—she turned to Rolf—"for its achievement."

Both gentlemen sprang up, Rolf bringing forward Miss Hoborough's favourite chair, Lord Medhurst taking her hand and voicing his satisfaction in seeing her sufficiently restored to leave her own room. She acknowledged this with a slight smile and a polite enquiry as to his own health, but as soon as she could in courtesy do so, turned again to Rolf.

"I have been talking to your mother," she told him. "Why did you not tell me that you and Charmian were promised? You must have known the match would have had my full approval. Oh, yes! Mary tried to explain that you all shrank from the thought of depriving me of my new-found niece

217

when we had only just met. Well meant, no doubt, but foolish."

The delivery of this rebuke seemed to have a heartening effect upon the speaker. She lifted her head with all the old air of authority as she went on, "Your father's assumption is perfectly correct. I *do* want this affair hushed up. But I shall take all due precautions for the future, even though common sense suggests that a second attempt is extremely unlikely. I have sent for Hogan. Stanton may remain in Ireland or travel abroad as he wishes, but his allowance will continue only so long as he stays out of England, and his income will be left in trust after my death on the same terms. Hogan will see all made safe. And I shall also lodge a full account of the recent happenings with him. For the rest, it will be for you to guard your wife. Perhaps, when she is a little stronger, you will bring her to visit me—either here or in Town. I shall hope and pray that her sufferings have not given her an ineradicable dislike for the place, since some day it will be hers. I would like to think of your children playing here, and growing up to be healthy, useful citizens. But now I am charged with a message from the redoubtable Susan, who says that you may go and sit with her nurseling for a little while, providing that you do not over-excite or tire her. I daresay planning her nuptials will do more to restore her than all the possets and panadas."

Susan had established her charge on the day bed

in the window embrasure, and although she had dressed the girl as though she was a babe, the process had tired her. She looked pathetically frail and defenceless, the long lashes sweeping her pale cheeks, slim scarred hands idle in her lap. Rolf's heart swelled with pity and tenderness.

"Beloved," he said gently.

The great dark eyes opened. She turned her head slightly and her hands flew to her breast as delicate colour flooded her cheeks. "Rolf!" she breathed, and cast aside the shawl that Susan had tucked about her, as she tried to struggle to her feet.

With deep thankfulness Rolf realised that the dreadful, half-crazed vacancy was gone, that her face was alight with love, and he folded her close as though he would never let her go. And she relaxed against him, her head on his breast, her hands coming up to clutch his lapels. He could almost feel the tension and the nightmare memories draining out of her as she snuggled childishly into his embrace. He kissed her lightly, and sat down on the day bed, still holding her in his arms.

"You will scarcely be surprised to hear," he began solemnly, "that after the fright you have given me I propose to marry you out of hand without further delay."

She clasped her hands happily. "Oh, thank you! I am so glad. How soon will it be?" she said eagerly.

That made him laugh despite his earnestness. "You make it sound as though I had offered you a high treat for your birthday—and you about seven years old," he teased her.

"Well so it is. Being married is rather like a birthday, isn't it? A new beginning. And to be spending the rest of my life with you is certainly my notion of a high treat."

He forgot to be gentle and hugged her fiercely. "And mine," he murmured against her lips. And thought how close they had come to losing it. But it would not do to be reminding her of grim events gone by. He said cheerfully, "Well, Papa has promised to procure the licence. Where would you like to be married?"

That called for some thought. Presently she said slowly, "I would really like Medhurst best, because I have always been so happy there. But if you will agree to it, I think it should be here. It would be something for my aunt to think about. She—she is in great distress, you know, though she hides it so bravely. And she has so little. Let her have the planning of our marriage. It is not very much, but it may give her some happy memories to season the bitter ones."

He raised her hands to his lips and kissed them gently. "My little Great-heart," he said softly, worshipfully.

She snatched her hands away. "Don't!" she choked. And then, at the surprise and hurt in his face, "Don't p-praise me. You d-don't know. I'm so sh-shamed." And, her fragile self-control shattered, sobbed bitterly.

He soothed her patiently, drying her tears, murmuring nonsensical love words that he had not dreamed he knew, until the brief storm subsided. She took the handkerchief from him and scrubbed her eyes fiercely, blew her nose and announced between a sob and a gulp, "I'm not a Great-heart. I meant to be. I t-tried to be. But I'm just a silly cry-baby. I d-don't deserve to marry you."

Rolf had not thought it possible that he could love her more. He wasn't even sure that it *was* love —this queer mixture of pity for her distress and tender amusement at her tragic face and words. He could only be thankful that she was his to kiss and to comfort—and that the means of comfort were ready to his hands.

"If it comes to a judgement between us," he suggested gently, "do you think that *I* deserve to marry *you?* It was my stupid pride that gave Hoborough his opportunity—that put you in peril of your very life. And I must go all my days in *that* knowledge. Isn't that worse than being—to use your own phrase —a cry-baby? Indeed, of the two of us, you are much the better bargain. If you had *not* been frightened, situated as you were, you must have been utterly lacking in sensibility, whereas there is no excuse whatever for *my* conduct."

This last she could not allow, of course, but she was so much struck by the masculine good sense of his other arguments that she presently allowed herself to be convinced. When he further suggested that they might as well make the best of a bad bargain and get married just the same, she actually chuckled.

"It would certainly be a pity," she agreed, solemn-faced, "to waste your Papa's efforts over procuring the licence. Or to deprive Aunt Tabitha of the pleasure of choosing my wedding gown." And held up her tear-stained face to be kissed.

MASTER NOVELISTS

CHESAPEAKE
CB 24163 $3.95
by James A. Michener

An enthralling historical saga. It gives the account of different generations and races of American families who struggled, invented, endured and triumphed on Maryland's Chesapeake Bay. It is the first work of fiction in ten years to be first on *The New York Times Best Seller List.*

THE BEST PLACE TO BE
PB 04024 $2.50
by Helen Van Slyke

Sheila Callaghan's husband suddenly died, her children are grown, independent and troubled, the men she meets expect an easy kind of woman. Is there a place of comfort? a place for strength against an aching void? A novel for every woman who has ever loved.

ONE FEARFUL YELLOW EYE
GB 14146 $1.95
by John D. MacDonald

Dr. Fortner Geis relinquishes $600,000 to someone that no one knows. Who knows his reasons? There is a history of threats which Travis McGee exposes. But why does the full explanation live behind the eerie yellow eye of a mutilated corpse?

8002

This offer expires 9/30/80

GREAT ROMANTIC NOVELS

SISTERS AND STRANGERS PB 04445 $2.50
by Helen Van Slyke

Three women—three sisters each grown into an independent lifestyle—now are three strangers who reunite to find that their intimate feelings and perilous fates are entwined.

THE SUMMER OF THE SPANISH WOMAN

CB 23809 $2.50

by Catherine Gaskin

A young, fervent Irish beauty is alone. The only man she ever loved is lost as is the ancient family estate. She flees to Spain. There she unexpectedly discovers the simmering secrets of her wretched past . . . meets the Spanish Woman . . . and plots revenge.

THE CURSE OF THE KINGS CB 23284 $1.95
by Victoria Holt

This is Victoria Holt's most exotic novel! It is a story of romance when Judith marries Tybalt, the young archeologist, and they set out to explore the Pharaohs' tombs on their honeymoon. But the tombs are cursed . . . two archeologists have already died mysteriously.

8000